All Family Ain't Good Family

Sometimes you have to play the hand you get

Mabel L. Johnson

Kim Y. Nelson

ALL FAMILY AIN'T GOOD FAMILY

www.ClarenceandLeePress.com
ISBN: 978-1-947922-01-3

DEDICATION

In loving memory of Mabel L. Johnson....

Acknowledgements

First and foremost, I would like to thank God for His constant presence in my life and His many blessings.

I would like to thank Ricky, Michael, Kenny, and JeCare' for their support.

Thank you to Allante', Talyr, and Mia for gracing the cover with your beauty.

Thank you to the staff at Akustic Kapsule, Inc. for your patience.

CHAPTER I

Meredith...

I awoke from a restless slumber, just as my cousin Johnnie pulled into Las Vegas. I sat up straight and turned my head from side to side, to get the crook out of my neck. My neck hurt and I was gasping for breath because of the hot dry air. But I didn't mind because I was in Las Vegas, the city of lights. Gene was still asleep beside me, so I sat there looking out at the view and thinking. I had heard that Las Vegas glittered at night. But even in daylight, it was the most beautiful sight I had ever seen. It was a far cry from Canton, Mississippi. The thought of being here filled my heart with delight.

This is the city Las Vegas, Nevada, my name is Meredith Jones and I'm going to live here, I thought to myself.

Although at that moment, I had no idea exactly where that was going to be. If I couldn't live with Alice or Ben, then I was going to be in trouble. After paying my cousin Johnnie twenty-five dollars to bring me, I only had six dollars to my name. He was under the impression that he was bringing me to live with my sister Alice. I had told him that she was expecting me because I was afraid that he wouldn't bring me if I didn't have a definite place to live. But I hadn't been in touch with Alice or my brother Ben in four years, so I didn't know if either of them had room for me. I had heard about them through my oldest sister Gloria. Ben and Gloria always kept in touch with each other. It was a solemn promise they had made to each other when Ben left Canton hitch-hiking, after his best friend drowned. He eventually ended up in Las Vegas, where he settled down and got married.

When Alice was in the twelfth grade, she got Ben's address from Gloria and started writing to him. After she graduated from high school, he sent her a bus ticket to come to Las Vegas. Later I heard from Gloria that Ben had put Alice out. Gloria said that Alice had started his two little girls to smoking. His oldest daughter Lucy was seven and the youngest Joyce was five. They both were hooked by the time he found out that they had been smoking. He was paying Alice to baby-sit the girls while he and his wife Laura worked. One Sunday while Alice was away Joyce wanted a cigarette. She tried to wait for Alice, but Alice was taking too long, so she walked up to Ben and said 'Daddy, I need a cigarette to charm my nerves.' After the initial shock, Ben questioned the girls and found out that they had been smoking ever since Alice had gotten there. He blessed Alice out, gave her some money, and put her out of his house. Now she had her own place and a job at a laundry. But that was all that Gloria knew about Alice's situation.

I graduated from high school in June of 1960, and a week later, I found a job at a diner on the outskirts of town. It was in walking distance from my house, where I lived with my grandparents. I could just walk straight up the railroad tracks. I was hired as a dishwasher and short-order cook. My shift was from ten o'clock a.m. to six o'clock p.m. and the salary was fifteen dollars per week. But I soon found out that the job description was a sham. What my boss Mrs. Grimes really needed was a maid. And her intention was to ease me into the position. On my first day there, I began to overhear whispers among the blacks. They would always stop talking and disperse whenever I came near; but not before I got a chance to overhear a little of their conversation. It had something to do with Mrs. Grimes' maid. Her name was Bessie Green, and something bad had happened to her. It made me feel bad that they wouldn't include me in on their conversation. So, I started standing back whenever they had their heads together. When I came in to work, I always smiled and spoke to them. But the only one who ever smiled back was Miss Emma, the head cook. I got the feeling that they didn't like me. So, I just did my work and stopped trying to fit in with them.

The workers were all afraid of Mrs. Grimes and her son Bobby because they were mean to them. They didn't allow their employees to talk unless it was about their work. And they talked to them any kind of way. The first week I was there, they put their best foot forward for my sake, but like my grandmother always says, 'A leopard can't change its spots.' So pretty soon, they were back to their old ways and I was included. One day, out of the clear blue, Mrs. Grimes told me that I was slower than molasses in the winter time. From then on, she had something mean to say every day.

One morning when I came in, Mrs. Grimes came back to the kitchen and asked me if I knew how to iron.

"Yes Ma'am."

"Then when it's slow around here, I'll be taking you over to my house to wash, iron and clean up."

"Yes Ma'am."

Miss Fanny and Miss Emma looked at each other funny. Then Miss Fanny told Mrs. Grimes to taste the spaghetti sauce that she was making. She dipped a little up in a spoon and tasted it.

"It's hot and spicy, just like I like it."

"Thank you, Ma'am," she said and started grinning from ear to ear.

As soon as Mrs. Grimes left, they had their heads together whispering about her. I was hoping that we would always be busy at the diner, so I wouldn't have to go to her house. By this time, I feared her and Mr. Bobby just like the others. But, I felt safe at the diner around Miss Emma.

Altogether, they employed five black females, two white females and two black males. The two males, Toby and Eddie, worked inside and cleaned up around the outside. Toby worked the same shift as Barbara and me, from ten until six. Eddie came on at three o'clock and worked with Lucille until closing time. The two cooks worked the morning shift. Mr. Bobby supervised Toby and Eddie when they worked outside. They were all twenty years old, but Mrs. Grimes told Toby and Eddie to call him 'Mr. Bobby.' We all had to call him 'Mr. Bobby.' He was a big fat slob with light brown kinky hair. And with Mr. George being his step-father, the help were always whispering that there was a skeleton in the closet.

When his mother wasn't around, there was nothing that he liked better than being with Toby and Eddie. As soon as she left the diner, he went out front where they were. If he was in a bad mood, he yelled at them and gave them orders. But if he was in a good mood, he would horse around with them. They would sing and do that dance called the Hand Jive. Toby could do the Hand Jive real good. We would watch them through the front glass window along with Mr. George and the two white waitresses. But when Mrs. Grimes caught one of us looking out of the front glass window, she would ask us if we had lost something out there. The only good quality she had was her generosity with her food. She was fat and she enjoyed seeing people feed their faces. She had a peephole at the waitress station that she used to watch her customers eat. She liked it when they cleaned their plates. All of the female help were fat and she was always trying to feed me. I weighed a hundred and five pounds and she was always telling me that a strong wind would blow me away.

***

The day that I had been dreading finally came. After lunch, she came back to the sink where I was washing glasses.

"Leave the glasses, Barbara can finish them. You go get ready so I can take you over to my house to iron. Mr. George and Mr. Bobby are about to run out of shirts."

"Yes, Ma'am."

I felt like I had just received a stiff sentence. Miss Emma and Miss Fanny looked at me. They knew something but they were too scared to tell me. I walked to the back of the diner and took off my apron. I got my purse and stood near the back door waiting for Mrs. Grimes. While I was standing there, I thought to myself.

I don't want to be her maid and she can't make me. I'll do it this time and then I'll just quit and find me another job.

She came through and told me, "Let's go."

I followed her out and got in the back seat of her four-door sedan. On the way over, she asked, "How do you like working at the diner?"

"I like it. And, I thank you Ma'am for giving me the job."

"How would you like to be my maid?"

"I don't know Ma'am. I don't know much about housekeeping."

"Bullshit," she scoffed. "You little colored gals are keeping house by the time you're knee high to a duck. Some of you have babies by the time you're twelve."

"I'd rather work at the diner."

We didn't talk the rest of the way to her house. When we got there, we got out of the car and she let me in. She showed me where the laundry room and the damp shirts were and said that she was going to take a nap. The ironing board was already set up and the electric iron was sitting on the board unplugged. I plugged up the iron and took a shirt out of the basket and laid it on the board. I kept touching the iron to see if it was getting hot, but it wasn't heating up. I wasn't familiar with the electric iron because we were still using the old fashioned smoothing iron. After I saw that it wasn't going to heat up, I went to her bedroom door.

"There's something wrong with your iron."

"What do you mean?"

"It's not heating up."

She jumped up and followed me to the laundry room. She looked at the iron and said "You didn't turn it on you nit wit."

She turned the iron on, set the dial and said, "Now let me rest. I have a headache."

She walked out and went back to bed. After a while, she called me and I walked down the hall to her door.

"Yes Ma'am," I answered cautiously.

"Bring me my Anacins from the kitchen counter and a glass of water. I took two Anacins, but I'm going to have to take another one. I can't shake this headache."

"Yes Ma'am," I said and walked back to the kitchen.

I had no idea what an Anacin was or what the word looked like. The only things that I'd seen used for a headache were Bromo Celsia, which we called B.C. Powder, and Chamomile flowers that we used to make tea. There were a lot of medicine bottles on the kitchen counter and after I got the water, I stood there fumbling through them. I was looking for the word 'Anderson.' But I didn't see anything that looked like that.

In a few minutes Mrs. Grimes called out "What in the hell are you doing in there? Bring me my Anacins."

"It's not in here Ma'am," I called to her.

"You're a damn liar!" she yelled. "I just set them up there."

She jumped up and rushed to the kitchen. I was standing at the counter holding the glass of water and trembling. She grabbed the Anacin container from the counter and shoved it in my face, touching my nose.

"What is this?" she yelled. "If it had been a snake, it would have bit you. Are you blind or just dumb? What did they teach you over there at that nigger school anyway? Now get back in there and iron those shirts. And you better not leave no wrinkles in Mr. George's and Mr. Bobby's shirts neither."

She snatched the glass of water out of my hand and some of it spilled.

"Get that up!" she yelled. "Or don't you know what a mop is?"

She went back to bed and I found a mop and mopped the water up. I put the mop back and started ironing the shirts. I didn't iron as many as I could have because I was too afraid of leaving a wrinkle in them. The ones that I did looked great and I was hoping that she'd be pleased.

In about three hours she got up. She called to me to get ready to go back to the diner. Before we left, she came in and examined the shirts. She hung the last one back on the rack.

"You're a dumb little shit, but you sure can iron. You can finish the others tomorrow."

On the way back, the only thing she said was, "Did you unplug the iron?"

"Yes Ma'am."

I didn't want to quit because I needed the money to help Mama. Out of the fifteen dollars I made each week, I always gave her eight and kept seven. When we got back to the diner, she went straight to the front and I put my apron on and went back to the sink. Miss Fanny and Miss Emma had left. And Toby was helping Barbara until I got back. In a few minutes, Mrs. Grimes came back to the sink where I was washing dishes and handed me a bottle of Coca Cola and a glass with ice. I didn't want the Coca Cola. But I poured some of it in the glass and drank it anyway because she stood there looking at me for a while. As soon as she left, I gave the rest to Barbara.

Mrs. Grimes must have said something to Mr. Bobby about me because he walked through to the back of the diner, then came back and stood by the sink where I was washing dishes. He stood there for a while looking straight ahead, then looked directly at me and walked away. That's when I decided, money or no money, I was going to quit.

I said to myself, "Working in the fields is better than this. At least I'm not always afraid."

When it was time for me to get off, instead of keeping my big mouth shut, I bragged about quitting.

"I will never set foot in this place again," I said to Barbara and Lucille.

When I didn't show up at ten the next morning, Mrs. Grimes kept coming back to the kitchen checking to see if I had come in. When it was obvious that I wasn't going to show up, she asked the others if I had said anything about not coming back.

Miss Fanny and Miss Emma said, "No Ma'am."

Then Barbara spoke up, and said, "She quit Ma'am."

Mrs. Grimes spun around and looked at her.

"You know that I've been looking for her all morning!" she yelled. "I should wring your black neck for not telling me this sooner. Toby did you know that she had quit?"

"No Ma'am," he said looking down.

"I know one thing!" she yelled. "I'd better start getting some loyalty around here, or the whole lot of you is going to be out looking for work! And you ain't going to find no place in town where the working conditions are as good as they are here! Mrs. Edwina, across the tracks, makes her help pay for every bite they put in their mouths. I give you all a freehand with my food, even with Mr. Bobby protesting all to hell. So, you all just better start showing me a little appreciation around here. Toby, do you know where Meredith lives?"

"Yes Ma'am."

“Well take my car and go get her,” she yelled. “Tell her that I said I’m sorry and please come back.”

She handed him her car keys and said, “Don’t you come back here without her.”

***

I was on the back porch washing clothes in a wash-tub with a wash-board when Toby drove up. I hadn’t planned on her sending anybody after me. I didn’t even care whether I got my last pay or not. She could just keep it as far as I was concerned. I wasn’t even going to pass by that place again. Not on the same side of the street anyway. I’d lead Mama to believe that I was off for the day. I was planning to go look for another job before I settled for going to work in the fields.

Mama came to the backdoor and said, “There’s a young man from your job here to see you.”

I thought Mrs. Grimes had sent Toby to bring my last pay.

“Did he say what he wanted?”

“No, he just asked to speak with you.”

I walked through the house and out to the front porch. Toby was sitting on the edge of the porch. I spoke and sat down beside him.

He smiled and asked, “You know why I’m here don’t you?”

I looked at Mrs. Grimes’ car parked in front of my house and answered, “I have a good idea, but go ahead and tell me anyway.”

“Mrs. Grimes sent me here to get you,” he said. “She told me to tell you that she’s sorry and to please come back. I really think she means it. You should have heard what happened in the kitchen this morning.”

“What happened?”

“She really let us have it.”

He told me everything that she’d said to Barbara and the others. I laughed when he told me about the working conditions being better there. And I made a joke.

"Well if her place is the best in town, the other places must be ran by Satan himself," I said.

I thought it was a pretty smart remark, but Toby didn't laugh. I guess he was being loyal.

I sat there for a while without talking to him. Then I said, "Okay, I'll go back this time, but she better not never call me dumb or a nigger again. Wait here, I'll get ready."

"Okay, but please hurry."

I went to my room, changed clothes and combed my hair. Then I went to the kitchen and told Mama that I was going in to work because they were short-handed. I got my purse and walked out.

"Let's go," I told Toby.

"Okay," he said happily.

On the way, he loosened up and told me about some trouble that he'd had with Mr. Bobby.

"You think that you all got it bad. But Mr. Bobby is crazier than his momma. One day I was stooping over picking up trash and he walked up and kicked me in my behind as hard as he could. It hurt so bad, I wanted to cry. But I wasn't going to give him that satisfaction. I got up off the ground and laughed and pretended that it didn't hurt me. But after that, I made me a stick to pick up the paper. It has a sharp point."

"I saw you with it."

"And you just let him do it again. I'm going to stick him right in that big gut of his."

"But you know that they would call the law and have you arrested."

"They will have to catch me first because I'd be on my way to Chicago. I'm going to Chicago anyway, just as soon as I save a little more money. If you save your bus fare, you can go with me."

"No thanks."

"Well the offer is still good if you change your mind, because Mr. Bobby and Mrs. Grimes are stone crazy. Mr. George is okay but he's half drunk most of the time."

When we got to the diner and I walked in, the first words out of Mrs. Grimes' mouth were, "Meredith are you hungry?"

"No Ma'am. I've had breakfast, thank you."

"You all hurry up with those glasses," she said to the others. "We're just about out."

She left and went back up front. Toby stayed outside and gave her the car keys through the front door. Later I saw her outside talking to Toby and I was glad that I hadn't said more.

For the next few days, they were nice to all of us. And in the following week, Mr. Bobby didn't come in at all for two days in a row. Mrs. Grimes opened the diner and left. And then Mr. George was in charge. I figured that Mr. Bobby was probably sick, but I didn't ask. Whatever the reason was, I was just glad that they were gone. Even the two white waitresses, Dell and Sue, were relaxed and friendly. Miss Fanny cooked up some fried chicken backs and gravy and steamed some rice. We were all licking our fingers, including Mr. George, Sue and Dell. The next day she used some chicken feet and made chicken and dumplings. Once again, we all ate together.

Mr. George was so different from them. We wondered how they ever got together. He was such a kind man. He was thin, red-headed and about 5'6" tall. He was at least two inches shorter than Mrs. Grimes. He came from somewhere on the east coast, either New York or New Jersey. You could tell by the way he talked. He was a very good handyman. He did most of the repairs around the diner and even closed the diner at eleven o'clock p.m. That is when he was sober enough. But they didn't allow him to have money in his pocket because whenever he got his hands on some money, he got drunk. So, he was more like a servant working for his keep. Once in a while, he would defy them and take money from the cash register or just not ring up a sale. Then we wouldn't see him for a couple of days. And when he did show up again, he would have a black eye or bruises on him. Sometimes they'd throw him out of the house and make him sleep in his car.

We all enjoyed ourselves for two days. But the following day the mother and son duo were back and everything was quiet again. That Friday morning when I got to work, Mrs. Grimes was in the kitchen. I walked in, and put my purse away and started putting on my apron.

"Toby will help out in here. I need you at my house to clean up. My house is a mess. If you're hungry, Fanny will fix you some breakfast. Then Mr. George is going to drop you off at the house."

"Yes Ma'am."

She went back up front and Miss Fanny asked me, "What do you want to eat?"

"Nothing. I'm not hungry."

I sat on a bench by the back door and waited for Mr. George. After a while, he walked through.

"Are you ready?"

"Yes Sir."

I got up and followed him out to his car. He opened the door to the back seat for me, and I got in.

Well at least I'll be at the house alone, since Mr. Bobby is in the front of the diner.

When we got to their house, Mr. George unlocked the front door, let me in, and left. I walked down the hall to use the bathroom. The door was ajar, so I pushed it open. I gasped when I saw Mr. Bobby standing over the toilet. His pants were down and he was pulling up his stomach. He looked up.

I backed away sobbing, "I'm sorry."

"You black bitch! I'll kick your nigger ass!" he yelled.

I turned and ran towards the front door. He grabbed the toilet bowl plunger and threw it at me. It hit my shoulder just as I opened the door and fell through it. I could still hear him cursing at me as I got to my feet and ran down the street.

A fairly large strip of land separated their house from their neighbor, Mrs. Vera Cox. I ran down to her house and along the side of it until I reached her back door, because most whites don't allow blacks to enter their home through the front door. Mrs. Grimes didn't mind if you worked for her. I knocked on the back screened door and Mrs. Cox opened it.

"Come in child. What ever happened to you?"

"Mr. Bobby hit me," I sobbed. "I want to call Mrs. Grimes to come pick me up."

"Please come on in."

She gestured for me to go into the room where she had been sitting. She looked out of her window that was facing the Grimes' house, then came in the room and told me to have a seat.

"Can I get you a cup of tea?"

"No Ma'am. I just need to use your telephone."

"First let me get you a glass of lemonade. I'll have one too and we'll talk."

She came back with two glasses of lemonade and handed one to me. Then she sat in a chair near me. I took a sip of my lemonade, and then held the glass between both hands because they were shaking.

"Tell me exactly what happened."

"I walked in the bathroom on Mr. Bobby. I didn't know that he was home."

"But his jeep is parked right over there."

"I know that now. But I didn't notice it at first because I thought that he was at the diner."

"What was he doing when you walked in on him?"

"He was just standing there over the toilet with his pants down."

"I see. He probably thought that you saw his affliction. And that's why he got mad and hit you."

"What affliction?"

"First, I must remind you that you mustn't repeat a word I'm saying. I'm going to tell you this so you won't stay around there and get hurt, or worse. If you tell, it will cause trouble for you. That boy Bobby is a very bitter person because he was born without a penis. Before the doctors made him one, he had to pee through his butt. Judith took him all over Mississippi and Louisiana until she found a doctor that could help him. She finally found a surgeon in New Orleans who made Bobby a penis using skin and tissue grafts from other parts of his body. I wish that you'd got a chance to see it, so you could tell me what it looks like."

"I honestly didn't get to see nothing."

"That boy and Judith are lunatics. And they should be locked up before they kill somebody. What did he say to you?"

"He called me a black B and told me that he would kick my nigger A."

"He should be ashamed of himself. He passes for white, but he's the same as you."

"Really!?" I asked excitedly.

"He certainly is. Bobby's father is a mulatto. He was Judith Grimes' parents' house boy. When her father found out that she was in the family way, she helped the boy to escape and then ran away herself. And she came here to Canton. While she was away, her father contracted Tuberculosis and her mother caught it from him. They died about a year apart. There were just two children, Judith and her younger brother. The two of them inherited a lot of money and all the property. Judith went back to the Delta for a while after her daddy died. That's where she got the money to buy that diner and her place over there. Did they tell you what happened to Bessie Green?"

"No Ma'am. Nobody will tell me. They stop talking about it whenever I come around."

"I hope you'll have as much sense as they have and keep what I'm telling you to yourself."

"Yes Ma'am, I swear that I will."

"You're a very pretty girl," she said smiling.

"Thank you, Ma'am," I said smiling.

"I don't want to see the same thing happen to you that happened to poor ole Bessie Green. That poor soul left there in an ambulance."

"Do you know what happened?"

"Well, Judith and I had long stopped talking. But I heard from a reliable source that Bessie broke an antique vase. It was an heirloom that Judith inherited from her parents. It had been in her mother's family for over fifty years. Bobby held Bessie while Judith beat her until she passed out. Then they poured water on her to try to bring her around. But she had gone into a diabetic coma. George called an ambulance to take her to the hospital. They haven't had a maid over there since then. George is a nice man. The only harm that he does is to himself with all that drinking. He was a vagrant when he and Judith met. He wandered into the diner one day and ordered a cup of coffee. They struck up a conversation and she ended up bringing him home. She cleaned him up and hired him as a handyman around the diner. He's real good. He used to do work around here for me."

"I know. He does all the repairs around the diner."

"Six months after they met, they were married. Before they got married, whenever he got drunk they'd just let him sleep it off. But soon after they were married, all hell broke loose. When he came home drunk, they'd beat him and kick him out and make him sleep in that old tool shed out back. They still treat him that way now."

"Judith and I were friends when she first moved over here," she said. "But that was before I found out how she treated her help. When I spoke to her about it, she looked at me and said, 'They don't have feelings like we do. I heard my daddy say so.' I wanted to ask her if she thought that Bobby had feelings like us, but I didn't. I just stopped going around her and just talked to her whenever she called me."

"But after Bobby and another boy killed my dog, we became bitter enemies," she said. "Bobby and the boy bragged to a young girl about killing my dog. The girl told her mother and her mother told me. When I told Judith, she took Bobby's word over mine and the young girl's. Judith said that we were all lying on Bobby. I've never had a child, so that dog was my child. He was a gift from my late husband. He was all I had left."

"I'm from New York City. I was born and raised there," she said with a faraway look. "My late husband Albert inherited this place from his parents and brought me here. It was so different from the hustle and bustle of New York City that I just fell in love with it. It was nice back then. The children and the pets ran free. There was nothing to bother them. Then the families started selling out and moving on. And strangers started moving in. I just didn't have the heart to leave. I guess I'll die right here. I'm too old to be moving around now. But you should leave here. Have you finished up yet?"

"Yes Ma'am. I graduated this June."

"Then you should go up to New York or Chicago and find work."

"I don't know nobody in neither place."

"It was just a thought. But there are other jobs. You don't have to stay around there and let them hurt you."

"You're right Ma'am. I'm going to quit today. I'm not going to tell her. I'm just not coming back."

"Well, it was very nice to meet you and take care of yourself. And remember what I told you is just between us."

"It was nice to meet you too. Thanks for the lemonade and for talking to me. You have my promise. I won't mention a word to nobody."

She made a gesture toward her telephone and said, "You can go ahead and call Judith now."

I called the diner and Dell answered the telephone. "Judith's Home Cookin."

"This is Meredith. Let me speak to Mrs. Grimes please."

I heard her tell Mrs. Grimes, "It's Meredith and she wants to speak to you."

"What is it with that little twit now?" she asked, as she took the receiver. "What? No, don't tell me, let me guess. You don't know what a vacuum cleaner looks like do you?" She asked it in a loud mocking voice and then laughed.

"Mr. Bobby wouldn't let me clean up. He hit me and made me leave."

"Then where are you calling me from?" she snapped.

"I'm over at Mrs. Vera Cox's house."

"I'll be right there. And I better not find out that you've been over there blabbing."

"No Ma'am, I haven't."

She slammed the receiver down.

I hate the day that I walked into that place.

I hung up the receiver, and thanked Mrs. Cox again and told her that I'd wait outside for Mrs. Grimes.

"Good luck to you," she said, and let me out of her front door.

I didn't have to wait long before I saw Mrs. Grimes come speeding down the street. She stopped right beside me and yelled, "Get in!"

I got in on the back seat and she turned around in the middle of the street. A carload of young white boys almost hit her car. They yelled to her to watch what she was doing.

"Stay out of my way you little fools," she yelled back.

She turned into her driveway and stopped. Then looked back at me.

"Why did Mr. Bobby hit you and make you leave?"

"He was in the bathroom and I didn't know it. And I walked in on him."

"Did he hit you with his fist?"

"No Ma'am. He threw the toilet bowl plunger and hit me on my shoulder."

She got out of the car and told me, "Wait here."

She went inside and stayed about fifteen or twenty minutes, then came out looking angry. She got in the car, backed out and started back to the diner. She looked over her shoulder.

"Did Mr. Bobby hurt you?"

"Just a little. But it feels better now."

"I forgot to check my almanac," she said shaking her head. "It must be a full moon. Everybody's cutting up. Barbara came in again with liquor on her breath. She's broken two glasses already. I told her, if she breaks anything else, I'll kick her out of that back door so fast, she'll think lightning struck her."

I knew that she was telling the truth about Barbara because I'd smelled liquor on Barbara's breath many times myself. She offered me a drink once, but I told her, 'No thanks.' 'You need a little nip to work in this hell hole,' she said. But the liquor made her mean. She acted up in the evenings when Mrs. Grimes and Mr. Bobby weren't there. She did things real sloppy. She even made hot grease from the grill splash on me a couple of times. She'd push me aside and tell me that I was moving too slow.

"You know I've got a good mind to wring your black neck," she said looking back at me again.

"What did I do, Ma'am?" I asked surprised.

"I should wring your neck for running over there and telling old crazy Vera Cox about what's going on in my house."

Now ain't that the pot calling the kettle black. You all are the ones who are crazy.

"Do you hear me talking to you!?" she yelled.

"Yes Ma'am. I heard you. But I didn't tell Mrs. Cox nothing. I just asked to use her telephone."

"Do I look like a damn fool to you!?" she yelled.

"No Ma'am, you don't."

Yes you do. And you act like one too. I wish I had never met you or your crazy son.

"I know you told her something," she yelled. "But, I better not ever hear anything about it or I'll skin your black ass. Do you hear me!?"

"Yes Ma'am."

"I'll break that shoulder that Mr. Bobby hit you on!"

When we got to the diner, we got out of the car and went in through the back door.

"I'm going up front to get your money."

I thought she was about to say, 'And you're fired.'

"You can have the rest of the day off. But, I want to see you in here at ten o'clock sharp tomorrow morning."

"Thank you, Ma'am."

When she passed through the kitchen she told Miss Fanny to feed me. Miss Fanny came to the back looking sad and asked me, "What do you want to eat? I'll fix you anything you want. Mrs. Grimes has okayed it."

"Thank you, Ma'am. I'm not hungry."

Mrs. Grimes came back through and handed me a small brown envelope. I could feel the bills folded up inside.

"Thank you, Ma'am. I'll see you all tomorrow."

"I'm sorry about what happened."

"I'll be all right," I said with a fake smile.

I walked out the back door and looked back. I felt relieved that it was over. I had no intention of ever going back there. And, I wasn't ever going to allow anybody to talk to me like that again.

CHAPTER II

Mossy…

I was the youngest of my parents' six children, and the only one who was still living at home. I had two sisters and two brothers living in the West, and Ellen, the knee baby, lived in Dallas. That was where I was planning to go as soon as I had graduated from high school and made a little money. There was an eleven-year gap between Ellen and me because when she was five years old, my daddy got put into the penitentiary, supposedly for cattle rustling. He was in there for five years before my mother and brother, Robert Jr. found a reputable lawyer to get him out. The other lawyers just beat my Mama out of a whole lot of money and land. By the time Daddy was freed, our fifteen acres of land outside of Marlin had dwindled down to five. He and Mama had worked all of their young lives to buy that land.

Shortly after my Daddy got released from the pen, Mama got pregnant with me. She told me that when I was born, I looked just like Daddy's sister Mossy, so Daddy named me 'Mossy' after her. As I grew older, I could even see the resemblance between Aunt Mossy and me. I looked more like her than I did Mama and Daddy. And, I was going to be tall like her. By the time I was six, I was already tall for my age. I had gotten my hair, skin and figure from Aunt Mossy, but I had inherited my oversized breasts from my mother's mother. They started sprouting out when I was in the third grade. And over that summer, they grew by leaps and bounds. When I started the fourth grade, I was well endowed. I was the only girl in the fourth grade class with a full set of titties. The girls in my class admired my breasts. They asked me how I made them grow so large. I told them that they just grew on their own. But I hated my breasts because big boys and men would stare at me and the boys in my class had begun to tease me. Sometimes when the teacher left the classroom, the boys would put two big balls of paper or something under their shirts. And the other children would look at me and laugh.

One night I thought about an old Chinese custom that I had heard some older women talking about. They said the Chinese women used to bind the young girls' feet to prevent them from growing too large. So, I decided to bind my breasts to stunt their growth and to make them less visible. The next morning as soon as I heard Mama's truck leaving, I got busy. I'd heard her talking to Daddy and assumed that they'd left together because I didn't hear any movement in the house. Sometimes, when he was feeling well enough, he would go into town to help her peddle the farm goods. I went out to the kitchen, and took Mama's cheesecloth from the cupboard. I unwrapped the cheesecloth and measured it around my breasts. I took the scissors and cut off a piece long enough to wrap around my breasts two times. I put the cheesecloth back and found some safety-pins. Then I went back to my room and stripped down to my panties. I was standing in the front of my bureau mirror binding my breasts, when I heard footsteps. I looked up and Daddy was standing in my bedroom door. I jumped and grabbed a piece of clothing from my bed and covered myself.

"I didn't know that you were here."

He stood there looking at me for a few seconds.

"Be sure you feed those dogs before you leave here."

"Yes Sir. I will."

He walked away. But I didn't move until I heard the back door slam. I still didn't understand how he had sneaked up on me without me hearing him.

After he left, I finished binding my breasts and got dressed for school. I didn't have time for breakfast, so I gave Betsy and Red the plate of food that Mama left in the warmer for me, in addition to the cornbread and scraps that I usually fed them. I gave them water, closed the doors, and left for school.

The binding worked. My teacher and my classmates took a second look at me. One girl said that she knew my breasts weren't real in the first place. She was convinced that I had been stuffing my bra all along. I didn't care what she thought as long as my breast looked smaller. It seemed that everybody noticed the change except Mama. She acted so indifferent toward me that I spent my whole childhood life trying to figure her out. She wasn't at all mean to me. And, she gave me most everything that I asked for. But, she just didn't pay any attention to me. She'd wash and iron my clothes and put them in my room and I chose what I wanted to wear. She never made a comment, one way or the other, about what I had on. It was Ellen who was more like my mother until she moved away.

She graduated from high school and moved to Dallas when I was seven years old. I cried for days after she left. And when she came to visit, I begged her to take me back to Dallas.

"I can't," she said rocking me. "Mama and Daddy need you here."

"Mama don't need me," I cried. "She doesn't care about me. Go ahead and ask her."

"Don't say that because it's not true. Mama loves you."

But that was the way I felt. I thought that she didn't want me because she was tired after raising all of the other children. I was just there in her way.

After Ellen left, I started hanging around Mama trying to make her notice me. And that's when I started noticing her peculiar behavior, like bouts of crying and talking to herself. I was glad when Aunt Florence, her older sister, was around to keep her company. Aunt Florence lived down the road from us, but she didn't come around often because she didn't like Daddy very much. She always said that he was a poor excuse for a man and that he should still be in the pen. She didn't believe that he was sick. She thought that he was just trifling, although she was always claiming to be half sick herself. He didn't like her much neither and would rather that she didn't come around at all. But they always said a few words when she did come to see Mama.

After Daddy saw me naked that morning, he often passed by my bedroom door and looked in. And when he'd be talking to me, he'd look down at my breasts. Whenever he got the chance, he'd let his arm brush against my breasts. I tried to wrap my breasts even tighter so he wouldn't have anything to brush against.

The next time Ellen came to visit, she noticed that I had bound my breasts and called me to her. She felt my breasts. "Can't you see that Mossy needs a brassiere?" she asked Mama.

"I don't know nothing about buying no brassiere for a nine year-old child," Mama told her.

"Then let's go to town and I'll buy her one," Ellen said grabbing her purse.

The three of us went to town and Ellen picked me out two white cotton brassieres and Mama paid for them. The brassieres didn't work as well as the binding, but they did help a little.

Ellen slept with me while she was home, and I felt so safe. I had begun to feel uneasy around Daddy, so I stayed away from him as much as possible. I wanted to tell Ellen what he was doing, but I thought she would think that I was making it up so she would take me to Dallas. I decided to keep it to myself and make sure we weren't ever alone.

That turned out to be the wrong thing to do. Keeping what he was doing a secret gave him the courage to do the unthinkable. It happened on a Saturday morning right after I turned ten. Mama got me up early to help her load the vegetables and things on the truck because Daddy was ailing again, to let him tell it. After I finished helping Mama load the truck, she gave me a list of chores to do and left for town.

I did the outside chores first and then went in and ate breakfast. Daddy was still in bed, so I went to the bedroom door and asked him if he wanted me to fix him something to eat.

"Not right now. I'll get up in a minute and get something."

So, I went on and washed the breakfast dishes and scrubbed the kitchen floor. After I finished, I went to my bedroom and closed my door. I opened my window and took out my cut-outs. That's what Ellen called the paper models we played with. We'd cut them out of the Sears and Roebuck catalogs and magazines that Mama brought home. Ellen's cut-outs used to live between the pages of the magazines. But I'd moved up in the world. Mine lived in shoeboxes. I sat on the floor in front of my window and started playing.

After a while, I heard my bedroom door crack. I turned around and saw Daddy. He walked in with his pants unzipped and sat on the side of my bed where I was playing. Fear mounted up in me. But, I kept right on talking to my cut-outs, only louder. He started playing with my hair and said, "You're just gonna sit there and igg me, huh?"

"No, Sir. I'm playing."

"Stand up." When I did, he pulled me between his legs.

"You're so beautiful. You look just like Irma when she was young."

"I don't look like Mama. I look like Aunt Mossy."

"You use to. But here lately, you've started looking like your mama."

He held me closer.

"Please, let me go," I begged. "You're hurting me."

He ignored me and kept playing with my hair and rubbing my face. His hands felt rough and callused and I wanted him to take them off me and let me go.

"Please let me go," I told him again.

He laughed and said "I want you to show me your brassiere."

"I don't want to," I said and started crying.

He started feeling my breasts and I tried to pull away. He held me tighter and stood up, picking me up with him. He threw me on my bed and held me down with the weight of his body. I started kicking and hollering.

"I'm going to tell Mama."

"You better not tell nobody! You better not tell your Mama, Ellen, or Florence. If you do, I'll kill you. I brought you into this world and I'll sure take you out. Do you hear me?"

I didn't answer him, but I stop trying to fight him. I was afraid that he'd kill me right then if I made him mad. I lay still while he undressed me. I was wishing that Aunt Florence would show up and catch him herself.

He stripped me naked, and threw my clothes on the floor. And then he pulled his pants down. I kept reminding myself not to scream, so he wouldn't kill me to shut me up. But when he forced himself into me I started screaming and fighting. Betsy and Red were whining and barking outside of my window so he reached down and grabbed my panties off the floor and stuffed them in my mouth. Then he put all of his weight on me. I tried to turn my head to the side to get some air but I couldn't. The lack of air, the pain and the pressure of his body caused me to pass out.

When I came too, I was washed up, dressed and under a clean sheet. My pink bedspread was gone and I never saw it again. I got out of bed and started to the bathroom. I was in so much pain that I was doubled over. I heard Daddy coming so I crawled back in bed and covered up. He came and sat down on my bed and I felt the pain rip through my whole body.

"I'm sorry. I just couldn't help myself. But I meant what I said. I'll kill you dead as a doornail if you tell a soul."

When Mama came home, she came in my room and I pretended to be asleep. She laid a bag on my bed and left. She never even noticed that my bedspread was gone. She cooked and when supper was ready, she came to my door and called me. I was angry at her too, so I hollered back.

"I'm not hungry. I'm not ever going to eat again."

"What did you say?" she asked.

Daddy broke pass her and came into my room.

"Mossy get up and get ready to eat your supper."

"Yes Sir."

I got up and went to the bathroom. Then I walked to the table and eased down in my chair. Mama fixed my plate.

"I bought you two dresses. They're in the bag on your bed."

I didn't answer or look at her.

"Where are your manners?" Daddy asked.

"Oh, thank you Ma'am."

Daddy talked all through supper. He talked more than I'd ever heard him talk before. And he kept his eyes on me.

***

After he raped me, whenever Mama wasn't home, I'd half do my chores and leave the house. I spent a lot of time at Aunt Florence's and outside of my friend Dora Mae's house. She lived alone with her mother. Her father was dead and her grown sister and brothers lived in Chicago. Her mother worked for a white family during the day and came home in the evening. She wasn't allowed to let anyone in their house while her Mama was at work. So, we played outside and up under her house.

It was a long walk to her house so I started taking the short cut through a pasture. The pasture was land that once belonged to my parents. The new owner had a 'No Trespassing' sign posted, but my hounds and I would trespass whenever I deemed it safe. If the cattle were grazing at a safe enough distance and I thought that we could make it across, we'd go for it. But one day, I got careless and a bull came charging after me. Betsy and Red were off chasing something. But when I screamed, they came running and used themselves as decoys. They distracted the bull and let me make it through the fence. They were enjoying themselves though. They played that bull like a yo-yo. They had him going around in circles. After that, I started taking the long way around.

Dora Mae would always walk me part way home. And then, I'd turn around and walk her part way back. And she'd walk me part way back again. Sometimes, this would go on for a long time and my dogs would get tired of us and trot on home. It was as if they were saying enough is enough. You human beings are crazy. Dora Mae very seldom came to my house, but when she did, we'd go through the same routine, walking each other back and forth.

We always walked home from school together and in the past, we'd go straight home and do our chores. But when school started back that fall, I didn't always go straight home. Every morning I'd ask Mama if she had to go into town to peddle. If she said yes, I wouldn't come straight home. I'd stay away until I saw her truck. Daddy was ailing more and more and eventually stopped helping her to peddle.

Some evenings, after school, I'd slip right past my house and go over to Aunt Florence's. And some days, I talked Dora Mae into playing with me. When the weather was hot, we played down the road from the cemetery. It was nice and shady there. The trees from both sides of the road overlapped and the place was well groomed. It was an awesome sight. Daddy would get after me about not coming home. But it didn't do any good.

It was months before he got a chance to rape me again. Mama's first cousin Joseph died and Mama and Aunt Florence went to Louisiana for his funeral. I begged to go but Mama didn't want to take me out of school. So, I was left alone with Daddy for two days and three nights. He didn't bother me that first night. But, I was so afraid that he would, I had nightmares. I dreamed that a wicked witch had me locked up in a dungeon. The iron bars were far enough apart that I could reach my hand through them. And the witch was dangling a candy bar in the front of me. I reached for it but she kept it barely out of my reach. So, I gave up and sat down. When she saw that I wasn't going to let her tease me anymore, she brought the candy closer. I took it from her hand and the candy bar turned into a penis, and she started laughing. I dropped the thing and started screaming.

I woke up screaming and I woke Daddy up too. He jumped up and came into my room with his shotgun. I was sitting up in bed looking around.

"What's the matter with you?"

"Somebody was in here, but she's gone now."

"Will you open my closet?"

He cocked his shotgun and snatched my closet door open.

"There's nobody in here. What did you see?"

"I thought I saw an old woman. But I must have been dreaming."

He looked under my bed and checked my window before he left. He left my bedroom door open. And I was afraid of the witch and afraid of being raped, so I stayed awake as long as I could. But just before dawn, I fell asleep.

When my alarm clock went off, I was dreaming and thought it was the school bell ringing and I slept right through it. Daddy woke up and didn't hear me stirring, so he came and woke me up. He told me to go ahead and get ready for school and he'd do my morning chores. I hurried and got ready and left for school. I was feeling good about my Daddy. I'd forgiven him and was willing to let bygones be bygones. I was just glad to have my Daddy back. He'd tried to protect me. I decided that I wasn't going to play with Dora Mae after school. I was going home to do my chores and cook supper for him. Ellen and Aunt Florence had taught me how to cook. I was an expert with cornbread. It was the first thing that I learned to cook, because I had to cook it all the time for Betsy and Red.

When I got home from school that afternoon, I called out. "Hi Daddy, I'm home."

He was out back feeding the animals. I put my books in my room and started out back to tell him that I was going to do my chores and cook supper. But when I passed through the kitchen, there was a pot on the stove. I opened it and he was cooking black-eyed peas.

Oh well, I'll just make some cornbread. And today I will make it so good that it will melt in his mouth.

When I got to the back porch, he was coming in the house.

"Oh, I see that you came on home. Well, I've done your work and started cooking, so you owe me. And you've gotta pay up tonight."

I felt a lump in my throat and I got sick to my stomach. I thought about running to Aunt Florence's house. And then I remembered that she was with Mama. He read my mind.

"You'd better not leave this house this late neither. You remember what I told you I would do to you if you cost me a minute's worth of trouble."

"I'm just going to my room."

I went to my room and closed my door. I sat on my bed and looked at my books. I needed to study for a quiz the next day. But I knew that I wouldn't be able to concentrate, knowing what was awaiting me. I got in bed with my clothes on.

I hate him. And I'm going to kill him as soon as I'm big enough.

I lay there wondering if the same thing was happening to any other little girl. I wished that I was Dora Mae. Her daddy was dead. When he knocked on my door to tell me to come on and eat, I just about jumped out of my skin.

"Yes Sir," I answered. But I didn't make no attempt to get up.

When I didn't show up, he came back again.

"I can't eat."

"Why can't you eat?"

"I got hit in my stomach with a ball today."

"Who hit you?"

"A girl in my P.E. class. But she didn't mean to hit me. It was an accident. She threw the ball to me and I missed it."

He opened my bedroom door wide. "If you need to take something, let me know."

"Yes Sir."

My coming home early had paid off after all. He believed me so he left and didn't come back. I got up later and ate a peanut butter cookie that I had left over from my lunch tray. I took my clothes off, set my alarm clock and went to bed.

When I got up the next morning, Daddy was out in the barn feeding the livestock. I went out and fed the chicken, my dogs and milked both cows. Then I came back into the house and started getting ready for school. He came in a little later.

"How do you feel?"

"Just a little better. But I have to go to school, we're having a test."

He stood there looking at me.

"Excuse me."

I passed him and went to my room. I didn't see him when I got ready to leave for school. And I didn't announce that I was leaving. I just closed the front door and left.

After school, Dora Mae and I went to our special place. But I was quiet and irritable.

"Why are you in such a foul mood?"

"My cousin died. Mama and Aunt Florence went to his funeral."

"Well we can go on home," she said sadly.

So, we started toward home. We walked in silence for a long time. Halfway there, I grabbed her hand.

"Do grown men ever notice you?"

"What do you mean?"

"You know. Do they stare at you and make nasty comments?"

"No, not really. But I wish they did. I think about doing it all the time. I can't wait until I get grown. I'm going to do it every night."

"Not me. I've watched animals doing it and it looks disgusting."

"Why did you ask me that? Do men bother you?"

"Yes, sometimes."

"Girl, that's hipped!" she said excitedly. "But I know what it is. You see, you have a bosom and I don't. But I'm going to start massaging mine so I can catch up with you."

"I sure wish you would."

I asked her to walk to the store with me and she did. She didn't have any money, so I gave her a dime. We went in and I bought two bars of coconut candy, just in case I had to miss supper like I did the night before. We called the coconut bars 'A strip of lean and a strip of fat.' It was my favorite. It had four colors, a strip of red, yellow, white, and brown. And we use to say, 'A strip of lean and a strip of fat. And if you don't like that, you can have your money back.' She bought candy too and we went home.

When I got home, Daddy had cooked supper again. And he was sitting on the back porch doing something to his bridle. I went to the door and announced, "I'm home."

"Good. You can feed these hounds."

I mixed up the peas and cornbread from the night before and fed Betsy and Red. Daddy had done everything else including gathering the eggs, for which I was grateful. I hated going in that henhouse. It was nasty and it smelled bad.

After I fed Betsy and Red, I washed my hands and set the table. We sat down to supper.

"We haven't talked at length in a long time," Daddy said. "What's going on at school?"

The only thing that I could think to tell him was about a game we played. It was the game where the teacher would whisper something to the pupil in the front row. And that pupil had to tell the one behind him. And so on and so on until it got to the last pupil. And that person had to say it out loud, so the teacher could tell if the story was the same as it started out to be. Daddy laughed.

"Was the story the same?"

"It was nowhere close. My teacher said that it wasn't even on the same subject."

"What was it when it got to you?"

"The student in the front of me told me that there were thirteen original colonies. And that's what I told the student behind me. But when it got to the last person, it had changed to thirteen stars in the flag."

He laughed again and said, "That's how lies get started."

When supper was over, he left the kitchen and I cleaned up. When I finished, I went to my room and studied. When I got tired, I went to bed. I went to sleep feeling good because Mama and Aunt Florence would be home the next day. I was sleeping sound when Daddy got in bed with me and woke me up. When I saw him, I tried to get out of bed. But he grabbed me.

"You better not scream and act a fool like you did before. You're already broke in now and it's not going to hurt you if you be still."

I kept trying to get away and he yelled, "Don't make me mad!"

He pulled my night gown off and got on top of me. And I just lay there limp and let him have his way with me. He hurt me, but I didn't cry. I just gritted my teeth. I cried after he left my room. Later on, he came back to my door and reminded me that he would kill me if I told anybody on him.

He raped me every chance he got over the next four years. One time after he had raped me, I got so angry I lost my head.

"You'd better leave me alone and stay the hell away from me!"

"Don't you ever use that kinda talk with me! I'll let you slide this time, but if you ever do it again, you'll be sorry."

My menstrual cycle started when I was twelve years old. And after I found out that I could get pregnant, I tried harder than ever to keep him away from me. When he did get a chance to rape me, I was worried until my period came. Sometimes, I worried so hard that I dreamed of having a deformed baby.

One night I dreamed that I had a baby with a waterhead. And when I looked at it again, it had two hands on both wrists. I screamed and woke up Mama and Daddy. Mama got up and came to my room. She sat on my bed.

"What's wrong baby?"

"I had a bad dream," I answered and hugged her.

She hugged me back and I was so touched.

"Will you sleep with me?"

She smiled and covered me up.

"You'll be okay. I'll be back if you need me."

She left my room and barely closed the door.

As the years went by Daddy's health got worse. One time he tried to rape me and couldn't. He finally got frustrated and gave up. The only consolation that I had those days was that I knew I would get big enough to kill him some day. I had even mapped out a plan. I was going to shoot him with his own shotgun while Mama was away. Then I was going to get Dora Mae to run away with me and join the circus. I use to watch him using his shotgun, so I would know how to use it when the time came. He used to shoot black birds in our back yard and I'd watch. Once an opossum was in the henhouse, and he got his gun to kill it. I had to go with him, to hold the lantern. I watched every move he made and I was glad that the opossum got away. It was he who should have been killed.

I learned to cope with my situation by pretending to be two people. I was Mossy Lewis and Louise Lewis. It was Louise that Daddy was raping, and she always stayed home. Mossy went to school and played with Dora Mae. I was so good at it that Dora Mae never guessed what I was going through. We were friends right up to the ninth grade.

Then one evening we were walking home from school together and my mind wandered off. I had hastened my steps and was a few steps ahead of her. She had to struggle to keep up because she was short and bowlegged and sort of on the plump side.

"Wait up Mossy. Why are you walking so fast? You're walking all scatter-legged like you've been doing it."

I lost my head and turned around and flew into her. It happened so fast that she didn't know what had hit her. She didn't even try to fight me back. She ran away looking back.

"What did I do?" she hollered.

She kept a safe distance ahead of me until she reached her turn off. I hadn't meant to jump on her, but her remark hit too close to home. I just temporarily lost my head.

When I got home, I did my chores and then practiced walking correctly. I balanced my text book on my head and tried to walk like Evelyn Jackson, our home-coming queen. I knew something was wrong with the way I walked because somebody else had told me that I walked with my torso ahead of my feet. So, I practiced hard until I got it right.

After the fight, Dora Mae and I went our separate ways. I yearned for her friendship, but I didn't know how to tell her that I was sorry. She was different from the other girls that I knew. She was very unassuming. She used to say some of the funniest things. And she wasn't nosy and always asking a lot of questions. It hurt me to see her with other girls and I was alone. I didn't try to make friends with anybody else. I just kept to myself. I know she still wonders why I hit her.

The only other girl who tried to make friends with me had a bad reputation. There was a rumor going around that she was having sex with her grandfather, so I didn't want to be seen with her. I never stopped to think that maybe she was going through the same thing that I was going through.

CHAPTER III

Alice…

I often wonder what my life would be like now, if those little bitches of Ben hadn't told on me. Maybe I would be an artist. I become infuriated when I think about it. His wife and he kept them away from me that last week I was there. And, it was a good thing that they did. The little bitches told Ben that I started them to smoking, when in fact, it was vice versa. I hadn't thought about smoking until Joyce stole her kindergarten teacher's cigarettes and brought them home. After that pack was gone I bought cigarettes and gave them one whenever we were alone. Ben claimed that I had gotten them addicted to nicotine. He said his youngest daughter, Joyce, had a craving and that's why she asked him for a cigarette. But I know better, she was just being vindictive. She was the more spiteful of the two, and that was her way of getting back at me for breaking my promise to them.

I had promised to take them to the picture show after church. But instead I caught the bus and went alone. I decided that I wanted some time away from them. And it turned out to be the wrong thing to do. But she wasn't a bit more hooked than her sister Lucy or me. We only smoked cigarettes when we had them. Sometimes, we went a week or more without smoking and she didn't say a word about any craving. I didn't tell Ben that she'd stolen her teacher's cigarettes and brought them home because he would have just asked why didn't I tell them about it then. Besides, with him and Laura there to protect her, Joyce would have yelled out, 'You're just a lie.' That was her favorite phrase.

Ben was waiting for me that Sunday evening when I got home from the picture show and he lit in on me as soon as I walked through the door.

"I found out what you've been up too."

"What do you mean?"

"You got my babies hooked on cigarettes! How could you do something like that, as good as we've been to you?"

"What are you talking about?"

"You know perfectly well what I'm talking about!" he yelled even louder. "Joyce has a nicotine addiction! And she asked me for a cigarette!"

I looked around for the girls but they had them tucked away in their room.

"I don't believe this," I mumbled.

Ben kept right on yelling, "You're not fit to watch my girls! I don't even want you around them! You're too low-down and dirty! And I know where you got those old dirty low-down ways from too! You're just a chip off the old block!"

Until he made that last comment, I was standing there waiting to get a word in edgewise and to apologize for what I'd done. But his last remarks rubbed me the wrong way, because I knew that he was referring to our no-good daddy. Ben hated his guts and so did I.

So, I fired back, "Excuse me, but my ways are my own. My class motto was 'Don't be a carbon copy. Make your own impression.' And that's the rule that I live by, thank you very much."

I threw my head up and started down the hall to my bedroom.

"Not so fast! This matter is not over yet because you're not even sorry for what you've done! You're rotten to the core and I want you out of here!"

"Fine, I'll leave!"

I went to my room and sat on the bed. Ben jumped up and came to my door.

"I'll give you one week to find you somewhere to go. And, I'll give you some money when you find a place. Since you're so smart, you can make your impressions someplace else. You can't stay here because goodness knows what you'll have them doing next."

Fear and anger overwhelmed me and I started crying. He closed my door and left.

Where in the world can I go? I'm afraid to live by myself in a big city.

I could hear Lucy and Joyce in their bedroom talking and I said out loud, "How could those little bitches do this to me?"

I felt absolutely betrayed. I wished that they'd leave them with me just one more day before I left, so I could beat the shit out of both of them. Then, I would be ready to leave. I was the one keeping their secret and this is what it had come to.

When Ben sent me a bus ticket to come to Las Vegas, it was my intention to come here and find me one of those good jobs I had heard about back home. I was planning to work one year, and save enough money to attend art school. Lucy and Joyce's baby-sitter had just quit when I got here. Lucy told me that the baby-sitter said she didn't even want them walking on her side of the street. Laura's mama had been looking after them for the longest. But, she finally gave up and moved back to Louisiana, so she wouldn't be bothered with them.

So, Laura and Ben asked me if I would watch them until they found somebody and they would pay me. And I agreed to do it, but not because I wanted to. I felt obliged to do it because they were good to me. But Lucy and Joyce were the worst kids I'd ever met. I used to sit and watch and listen to them in amazement. They could beat any grown man or woman cursing and playing the dozens. They would face off and play the dozens on each other like it was a recital. I would just let them have at it until it came to blows. When one would out do the other one and the fighting started, I'd separate them and make them behave.

Joyce had the worst temper and the nastiest mouth. One day she told Lucy, "I hate to talk about your mammy. She's a good ole soul. She's got ninety-nine babies in her rubber asshole."

Mama used to say when somebody is talking bad about you, your ears will burn. *Laura's ears should sure burn behind that.*

***

That Fall, Lucy started back to school and Joyce started Kindergarten, so I told Ben and Laura that I was ready to start looking for work.

"We need you to watch the girls after school," Ben said. "And I'll raise your pay to twenty dollars a week."

Again, I agreed. About a week after they started to school, Lucy walked up to me and asked me if I could keep a secret.

"Sure. What is it?"

Joyce was standing there watching.

"First you have to cross your heart and hope to die if you tell," Lucy said.

"Okay," I said, crossing myself. "I cross my heart and hope to die, and go to hell if I tell. But how much of a secret can it be, if you're gonna tell me right in front of Joyce?"

"Oh, she already knows."

"Then what is it?"

"We have a whole pack of cigarettes. And we'll give you one, if you'll light one for us."

"Where did you all get cigarettes from?"

"Joyce found them on her teacher's desk."

"Where are they?"

She took them out of her dress pocket and handed them to me. I wanted those cigarettes for myself. But I knew that those little wenches weren't about to let me get away with that. I looked at those cigarettes and couldn't wait to wrap my lips around one. They smelled good and fresh.

"Will you do it?" Lucy asked.

I pondered the idea for a while and then decided what the hell? I'm gonna do it. They'll choke and I'll get to keep the cigarettes.

"Yes, I'll do it. But we're gonna have to smoke them out on the back porch, so your mama and daddy won't smell cigarette smoke in the house."

"Okay!" they exclaimed.

I got the matches and we went out on the back screened in porch. They stood around me while I lit the cigarettes. I put three in my mouth at once and lit them. And then handed each of them one. I kept the pack in my hand. That first drag tasted so good. I kept watching them for any sign of choking, but they were going at it like old pros.

"Have you all ever smoked before?"

"Plenty of times," Lucy answered.

"Where?"

"Over at the baby-sitter's house," Joyce said. "She used to light her cigarettes and forget about them, and we'd take them."

"Did you ever get caught?"

"Yes," Lucy said. "But we begged her not to tell. We told her if she didn't tell we'd be good. So, she didn't tell."

I didn't need to ask if they kept their promise, because I knew the answer to that. I sat there smoking and relaxing. My mind drifted back to the time when I first tried to smoke.

***

I made my cigarettes out of brown paper bags. My granddaddy caught me smoking once and told me if I ever did it again, he was gonna tell Mama.

"You could swallow a blaze," he said. "I knew a child that did it and it killed him."

I didn't stop. I just made Meredith watch out for me.

When we finished our cigarettes, I destroyed all of the evidence and gave them a piece of gum. I still had the cigarette pack in my hand. I was intending to keep it.

"Can we have our cigarettes back?" Lucy asked.

I gave them to her but I kept the matches out of their reach. A couple of hours later, I asked for another one.

"Okay, but you have to light us another one too," Lucy said. So, we all had another cigarette.

"I better keep them so Laura won't find them."

"Okay. But you better not smoke them up while we're at school."

I did smoke at least three the next day while they were at school. And when they got home, we all smoked together. We did the same thing the next evening until the pack was gone. After that, I started buying cigarettes for them and myself. This went on for months without Ben finding out until that Sunday evening when they told on me.

It took me a little over a week to find a place to move. During that time, Laura found an old lady from her church to watch the girls after school. I wasn't allowed to be alone with them anymore. Every evening, Ben would ask me if I'd found a place to live. And I'd answer, "No, I'm still looking."

The next Sunday, I walked to the church near their house. I attended that church because I had met a friend there, named Blanche. She was three years older than me and we hit it off the first time we met. She asked me to sit up in the balcony of the church with her. We sat there and talked all through the service. One of the things I found out was that she had a job and shared a two-bedroom apartment with another girl named Jean.

When I got to the church, Blanche was there. We went up in the balcony and started talking. I asked her if she knew of a room for rent.

"I've looked everywhere that I can think of. But I'm not having any luck."

"Why are you moving?"

"My brother is putting me out. I don't get along with his wife."

"I can't think of any place right off. But why don't you come and live with Jean and me?"

"Do you think that it will be all right with her?"

"Oh sure! She will be happy to be paying less for rent. Because then we will be splitting the rent three ways instead of two. And besides, it's my apartment. She's renting from me."

"How soon can I move in? And how much will my share of the rent be?"

"We'll work something out until you find a job. Maybe we'll let you pay the electric bill and buy your own food. I know your brother is going to give you something before he puts you out."

"He said that he would."

She wrote her address on a piece of paper and gave it to me.

"You can move in tomorrow. We get home from work about 4:30 in the evening. Jean has a car so we can help you to move if you like."

"I can manage. I'm sure my brother will be happy to help me get out."

"I'm sorry to hear that you all had a falling out. But I don't get along with my family neither, so I know how that can be."

"Thank you. But I'm sure my brother will come around."

When church was over, I walked home with mixed emotions. I was about to be on my own for the first time in my entire life and that part was scary. But on the other hand, I wouldn't have an adult figure to answer to. I could come and go as I pleased. A sensation ran through me when I thought about the fact that I could even have sex now.

All I have to do is to find somebody to do it with.

***

At Ben's house, the only things I did were cleaned up, watched those little half-raised bitches and go to church and to the picture show. I didn't even cook because Laura didn't want me to after I made cornbread.

When I first got to Vegas, she called me from work and told me to make some cornbread for dinner. I didn't know how to make cornbread, but I knew that Mama used meal, salt and baking soda. So, I found a large pan and poured some meal in it. Then I added two teaspoons of salt, two teaspoons of baking soda, and some water. I turned the oven on and put the cornbread in to bake. When Laura got home and saw it, she showed it to Ben and he laughed. But Laura got mad and told me to my face that their dog wouldn't even eat my cooking. So, the girls and I ate leftovers and sandwiches that night. Now that I was going to have my own place, I could start learning to cook and do anything else I pleased.

Ben, Laura and the girls were still out when I got home. As I approached the house, I said to myself, "I'm probably locked out."

But the key was in place and I unlocked the door and went in. I went to my room and started packing. I had to admit that I had a lot more than I had when I got to Las Vegas. I packed my things in two trunks. The only things that I left were my pictures of famous people on the wall.

When I heard Ben's car drive up, I went up front and sat on the couch. I was shocked when Lucy and Joyce walked right pass me without even looking at me. Let alone speaking to me. Ben and Laura had turned them against me just that fast. Before Ben could ask me if I had found a place, I beat him to the draw.

"I found a place today. You can fork over that dough you promised me."

"When are you moving?"

"Tomorrow evening!" I snapped. "Is that soon enough for you? Or you can fork over some extra and give me a lift to the hotel on the Set. I'm already packed and ready to go."

And then you won't have to keep your little bitches in seclusion.

I thought it but I didn't dare say it. I feared repercussion. Ben didn't play when it came to those little womanish girls.

"You can stay here tonight because Laura is off tomorrow."

"Big whoop-de-do! I get to sleep in the castle one more night."

Laura pretended to be busy in the kitchen, but I knew that she was listening. Ben took five twenty-dollar bills from his wallet and handed them to me.

"You know that you have a smart mouth. But you better watch it. You're not in the sticks anymore. You're in the West now and you're picking in the right cut to get your hundred."

"Speaking of a hundred, this is not enough," I scoffed. "I've got to pay rent and feed myself. And you know that I don't have a job. Now I know that a big-time spender like you can do better than this."

"You have two hands and two feet, so you can find a job. But that is all that I can afford right now. I'll give you some more next month, if you don't have a job by then. But I'm not going to be able to help you go to that art school, because we're putting the girls in Catholic school."

"I can make my own way thank you."

I got up and went to my room. I didn't come back out that night.

The next day, I caught the bus downtown so I wouldn't have to deal with Laura. I bought me two hot-dogs, a root beer float, and a used novel. I sat on the bench at the bus stop and read for a long time. At least four Westside buses came and went. I finally caught one back home. When I walked in the door, Laura asked me if I was hungry.

"No thank you. I ate downtown."

I went to my room and she followed me.

"I'm really sorry that things turned out this way. But I'm not holding a grudge and I hope that you won't. Because after all, we're still family. And Ben don't mean no harm neither. He just wants what is best for the girls. He's had a hard life and he is trying to make life easier for them."

"Spare me," I sneered. "I need a smoke."

I jumped up and brushed pass her. I went out on the back porch and lit a cigarette.

"If she comes out here, I'm gonna tell her what Ben has been doing and tell her that I helped him," I said to myself.

But she didn't bother me, so I kept my mouth shut.

***

When the girls got dropped off from school, they still didn't talk to me. And I knew that Laura was behind it. She was throwing a brick and hiding her hand by putting everything on Ben. I wanted both of them to think that they hadn't done nothing big by putting me out. So, when Ben walked in from work, I pounced on him.

"I'm ready to go right now and I need a ride."

Laura asked, "Can he eat his supper before it gets cold?"

"I need to go right now," I snapped. "I've got things to do."

"Who are you moving in with anyway?" Ben asked.

"Blanche Bennett. And she has a roommate."

"Blanche Bennett," he repeated out loud. "I've heard that name before, but I can't place it. Where does she live?"

I took Blanche's address out of my purse and read it out loud.

"Okay, we can go now."

"My trunks are in the room. They're too heavy for me to lift."

"I'll get them," he said, and went into my room.

He took one trunk to his car and came back and got the other one. I followed him out without saying a word to Laura.

We didn't talk on the way, because every time he tried, I snapped him up. When we got to Blanche's apartment, I got out of his car and knocked on the door while he was getting my trunks out of his car trunk. Jean answered the door.

"Hello. Is Blanche here?"

"Yes, she's here. You must be Alice."

"Yes, that's right. I'm your new roommate."

"Well come on in. We were expecting you."

Ben walked up and sat one of my trunks on the stoop.

"Well Benjamin Jones!" Jean exclaimed. "Where have you been keeping your good-looking ass?"

"I'd appreciate it if you didn't use that kind of language with me," he said, and went back to his car and got my other trunk.

"Oh, I forgot that you'd gotten religion."

Ben didn't answer her.

"Wait just a minute," I said. "Do you all know each other?" Ben looked at Jean and then said to me, "Take care of yourself."

Then he got into his car and drove away.

"Come on," Jean said. "I'll help you to get your things inside."

We carried my trunks inside together, one at a time.

"So, you're Ben's sister?"

"I'm afraid so."

"When Blanche told me that your brother was putting you out, I had no idea that it was Ben."

"So how long have you been knowing my brother?"

"I met him in 1953 when I first moved here from Oxnard, California. I was working as a maid at the hotel where he works. We became fast friends. He took me to the movie to see 'The Greatest Show on Earth,' but we fell out when he found out what I did besides making beds. My plan was to get rich quick, and he got on me about it. I told him that he couldn't tell me what to do because he was married."

I was about to ask her, "What is it you do?" but Blanche walked into the living room.

She had just gotten out of the bathtub. We spoke and hugged.

"I see you made it."

"Yes, I'll move these trunks as soon as you show me where I can put them."

"We'll put them in my room. You'll be sleeping on the couch until we can get a hide-away-bed for you."

"That will be fine," I said smiling.

"Guess who the brother is that put her out," Jean said to Blanche.

"Who?"

"Ben Jones."

"You never told me that Ben was your brother."

"I didn't know that you knew him."

"So, what did Ben have to say about you moving in with us?" Blanche asked.

I didn't want to tell her that Ben couldn't place her.

I just said, "There was nothing that he could say. He told me to get out of his house. So, it's not his business who I move in with."

"How old are you?" Jean asked.

"I'm nineteen. How old are you?"

"An old lady compared to you. I'm twenty-five."

"You're going to need a fake I.D. if you're going to hang with us," Blanche said. "I'll take you to get one on my day off."

“But why do I need a false I.D.? I’m plenty old enough to get a job.”

“But you can’t get into the nightclubs unless you’re twenty-one,” she said.

“I can see now that I’m gonna like it here.”

Blanche cooked and we ate and talked until real late.

The next morning, they got up and went to work. They worked as maids at the same hotel on the Strip. Blanche left her door key with me until she could get one made for me. When I got up that morning, I cleaned up the apartment real good so they would like me. We ate up everything that Blanche cooked the night before and there was no more food in the apartment. So, I got dressed and walked to a cafe on Bonanza Road. I ordered a steak and eggs and sat at the counter and had a conversation with the waitress. I liked my new-found freedom. I finished my meal and walked back home. That evening after work, Jean dropped Blanche off at home and she went on to her other job. While she was gone, Blanche told me all of Jean’s business.

The thing that Jean did besides making beds was prostitution and she gave all of her money to some dude named Jeff. Blanche was in the business also, but she claimed that she was choosy about who she went to bed with. And she didn’t give her money to her boyfriend, who she called Rooster. He gave her money and I could see that she was telling the truth. She wore expensive clothes and jewels, and she had expensive furniture in her apartment. All of the furniture in the apartment was hers. It was obvious that she had an expensive taste. She told me that the reason she didn’t own a car was because the one that she wanted cost $2,600 brand new. She didn’t have credit and hadn’t been able to save up that much at one time.

“I would rather walk than to drive a jalopy like that of Jean’s,” she said.

When Jean came home that night, her boyfriend Jeff was with her. She introduced us and I was smitten with his good looks. He was tall, slim and very handsome. I could see why she was giving him her money, if that was what it took to keep him. Jeff didn't stay long that night. Jean took him into her bedroom and closed the door. When he came out, he asked Blanche for a beer and left.

The next time that Blanche and I were alone, I asked her if Jeff was buying his own home because I wanted to know what he was doing with the money Jean was giving him.

"No. His car is larger than the shack that he lives in."

"Then what does he do with the money Jean gives him?"

"He gambles it off as fast as she gives it to him. He used to come here begging for food, so I stopped keeping food in the house. And, he's as stingy as hell. One night, Jean and I walked into the casino and he had a stack of silver dollars in front of him. Jean asked him for a dollar to get her a hamburger and he didn't want to give it to her. He told her to borrow a dollar from me. She got angry and yelled out, 'I'm not fucking Blanche.' I got away from them fast, so nobody would know that she was talking about me."

"Did he give her the dollar?"

"You better believe it. He gave her two. I don't care for the dude. I tolerate him because of Jean."

But nothing she said about Jeff changed my feelings about him. I thought that if I was given a chance, I could make him love me. I knew I could take his mind off gambling. I heard a preacher say that people gamble to fill a void in their life. I could fill Jeff's void if I ever got the chance.

A few days later, I met Blanche's old man, Rooster. He was so ugly I wanted to close my eyes. I had to admit that he did put me in the mind of a rooster. But he was real nice to Blanche. I guess that counted for something.

CHAPTER IV

Meredith...

When I got home, Mama was sitting on the front porch piecing a quilt. She smiled when she looked up and saw me. "Hi Baby. You're home early. How come?"

I didn't answer her right then. I walked over to her and sat down on the porch by her feet. I lay my head in her lap. She laid her sewing in another chair beside her and felt my forehead and the side of my face.

"Why are you home so early?"

"I have a headache," I mumbled.

She rubbed my forehead. "Raise up so I can go make you some tea."

"You don't have to get up. It will go away. I just need to rest here for a while."

By that time, the tears where rolling down my face and I didn't want her to see them.

"All right, but if you start to feel worse, let me know."

She started playing with my hair and it felt so good. She pulled a tress of it loose and wound it around her finger.

“Mandy’s boys and her daughter-in-law are here from Vegas.”

I raised my head up so fast that her finger got caught in my hair and I hollered, “Ouch! When did they get here?”

“Some time last night. They’re here for Esther’s funeral on Monday.”

Aunt Mandy was my grandparents’ oldest daughter. Miss Esther was Bertha’s mother and Bertha was my cousin Johnnie’s wife. Miss Esther lived out in Madison before she died.

“Have you seen them yet?”

“Yes. Mandy brought them over here right after you left.”

She took three silver dollars from her apron pocket and showed them to me. “Johnnie gave me these Bo dollars. And that boy Eugene sure is fat and pretty. He puts you in mind of a girl. He features Mandy so much. He looks like she just spit him out.”

As she was talking, a vision of the West was going around in my head. “How long are they going to be here.”

“I don’t know. But Esther’s funeral is not until Monday. I was so glad to see them, I forgot to ask. Bertha asked about you, and I told her that you wouldn’t be home until after six o’clock. She told me that Alice is doing fine, but she is wild as all get out.”

“Did they say anything about Ben?”

“Yes, she said that he and his wife are both working and they’re doing fine.”

“I want to go over there to see them.”

“Go ahead.”

“Where is Granddaddy?”

“He walked up to the store.”

“Has he seen Gene yet?”

“Yes, he was here when they came. Johnnie gave him three Bo dollars too.”

Gene was just one year older than me. And we were my granddaddy's fishing buddies before he moved out West. I picked up my purse from the porch.

"I'll be back."

"What about your headache?"

"Oh, it's much better now."

I almost ran the five blocks to Aunt Mandy's house. They didn't recognize me until I walked up on the porch.

"Hello," I said.

Bertha and Gene jumped up and hugged me at the same time. Johnnie stood there smiling until they turned me loose. Then he hugged me. Johnnie was so tall. I was hugging him around his waist. And he felt real thin. It seemed to me that Bertha and Gene were eating up all of the food. They both were plump. It felt good being around Bertha. I liked her a lot. I opened the front door and spoke to Aunt Mandy, and then sat on the porch swing with Bertha. She squeezed my hand and told me that she was so glad to see me. I told her that I was sorry about her mother. Aunt Mandy came out of the house and asked if we wanted something to drink.

Gene hollered, "Yes!"

She returned with four glasses on a tray and a pitcher of lemonade. She sat it on the cooling board and left. Bertha got up and poured us all a glass of lemonade. She sat back down and asked, "Did you take off work to see us?"

"I got off early. I didn't even know that you-all were here until I got home."

Gene cut in, "I saw Alice before we left. She looks just like a little painted monkey."

We laughed and I asked, "What do you mean?"

"She wears too much make up."

"Boy what's wrong with you?" Johnnie asked. "Don't you know that's Meredith's sister?"

"She knows that I'm just kidding. Don't you Meredith?"

"Yes. I don't mind you telling me how she looks."

"Why don't you move out there?" Bertha asked.

“I’m planning to as soon as I save enough money.”

“But that could take forever,“ Gene said. “Why don’t you go back with us? There is plenty of room. I had the whole backseat to myself on the way here.”

“But it’s not your car,” I told Gene.

“Johnnie don’t mind you riding back. Do you Johnnie?”

“If you can be ready by Tuesday morning, you’re welcome to ride back,” Johnnie said.

“How much will it cost me?”

“The going rate is thirty-five dollars. That’s what I’ve charged other people that I’ve taken back. But you can ride for twenty-five.”

Gene looked at me sad. “Do you have that much?”

“I’ve more than that.”

“Groovy,” Gene hollered.

“Are you going to live with Alice?” Johnnie asked.

“Yes. I got a letter from her. She’s expecting me.”

I was hoping that they didn’t know that I was lying.

Gene just looked down.

“Well now that all of that is settled,” Bertha said, “All you’ve got to do is get ready.”

I felt elated. I got up and poured myself some more lemonade. I drank it and sat the glass on the tray.

“I’ll see you all on Monday at the funeral,” I said.

“But I was planning for us to go downtown tomorrow,” Gene said.

“I can’t. I’m going out to Madison to visit Gloria this evening. I’m going to stay out there all day tomorrow. Because, if I’m at home, my boss will send somebody to get me. I’m not going back to work anymore.”

“Okay,” he said. “I’ll see you on Monday. But I’m going to hold you to your promise about going back with us.”

“I’m going.”

“Tell Gloria I said hello,” Johnnie said. “And tell her I’ll see her on Monday if not before.”

“Okay, I’ll tell her.”

I called to Aunt Mandy, thanked her for the lemonade and announced that I was leaving.

"You're welcome baby. Gene come help me in here."

I was glad that she called him because otherwise he would have wanted to walk me part way home, like we used to do before he left Canton. If I went over to their house he'd walk me part way back home. And when he came to see us I'd walk him part way home. But that day I wanted to be alone so I could think. My first thought was, "Go West Young Man Go West." But then my happy thoughts were overcome by gloom. I thought about having to break the news of leaving to my grand-parents. It wasn't going to be easy. Out of all their seventeen grandchildren, I was their favorite. They doted on me. And now, I'd have to tell them that I was moving thousands of miles away.

I was five years old when I came to live with them. My daddy left my sister Alice, who was four years older, and me in a house alone. And even before he left us he didn't take care of us. There was never any food in the house. I could still remember being hungry most of the time. When he did buy food it was just enough for one meal. It was either a can of pork 'n beans and a loaf of bread or a few slices of bologna and a loaf of bread. And we'd gobble it down in a hurry. Some mornings he'd get up before we woke up and slip away. On those days we didn't eat unless Gloria came by and fed us. Sometimes when we asked for food, he'd tell us, "Leave me alone and go suck your paws." Then one day we kept crying and begging for food until he got tired of us. He got dressed and put some things in a croaker sack. He told us that he was going to get us a hamburger. Alice asked him if we could have one each.

"You each can have one and some French fries."

We were so excited that we started dancing around. He left and told us to keep the latch on the doors. We watched him through the front window. He was trying to thumb a ride. When a pick up truck finally stopped and gave him a ride, we started jumping up and down and clapping our hands. We waited and waited for our hamburgers, but he never came back. We got so hungry that Alice showed me how to lick salt from my arm and then drink some water.

When Gloria came again, Alice told her that we'd been alone for three days. So, she got us ready and took us with her. But, we couldn't live with her because she lived in a rooming house. She fed us and took us to live with our grandparents. And I'd been with them ever since.

Now in three days it would all be over. I wished that I had a lot of money to give them, because sometimes money made people feel better. But I didn't have but ten dollars to spare, because after paying Johnnie twenty-five, I'd be practically broke. When I got home my grandparents were sitting at the table eating. I walked into the kitchen and handed Mama ten dollars.

"I forgot to give it to you before I left."

I walked over and kissed Granddaddy on the side of his face and said, "Hello."

"Thank you baby, I'll give you your change."

"No keep it. I gave it all to you."

"Your supper is in the warmer over the stove," she said.

"Thank you Ma'am. I've got to go wash my hands."

I washed my hands and took my plate out of the warmer and sat down with them. I tasted my food and told her that it was good. She liked for us to praise her cooking.

"Well thank you."

I looked at them and they looked so old and frail. And I remembered what she'd said about a person being "once an adult and twice a child." For a moment I felt like I was the adult and they were my children. And I needed to be there taking care of them. I felt like the weight of the world was on my shoulders. It must have shown on my face. Mama looked up and asked, "What is it baby?"

"Nothing."

"You've hardly touched your food," she said. "And I cooked the butterbeans and peach cobbler especially for you."

"I just drank too much lemonade at Aunt Amanda's. But I'm going to finish it."

I tossed my food around on my plate and asked, "Mama, what do you-all think about me going to Las Vegas to work?"

They both stopped eating and looked at me.

"I'm thinking about going back with Johnnie, Bertha and Gene."

Mama started to get up from the table, but Granddaddy Bailey grabbed her arm. "Essie, Meredith is grown. Let her go."

She snatched her arm away from him and yelled, "She's seventeen and what do you know!? I've heard about how it is out there. Most of the children are in gangs. And they're beating up and killing each other. Is that what you want for Meredith?"

"I don't believe that will happen to her. She has a good head on her shoulders."

Mama jumped up from the table and went to her room. Granddaddy shook his head and continued to eat. I got up from the table and went after her. She was sitting on the edge of her bed crying. I got down on my knees in front of her.

"Mama, please don't cry," I begged. "I've got to go. I'll send you lots of money back. I didn't tell you the truth about why I came home so early. Mr. Bobby hit me and I quit that job."

She stopped crying and asked "What do you mean about him hitting you?"

"I went over to their house to clean. And I walked in the bathroom on him and he hit me. I'm okay, but there's more. They're crazy Mama, and I'm afraid of them. You should hear the way that they talk to the colored people that works there. They've no respect for them."

"Why didn't you tell me this sooner?"

"I didn't want to worry you. I kept thinking that it was going to get better. But it kept getting worse. And there's one more thing. But you can't tell a soul that I told you except Granddaddy."

"I won't," she promised.

"They had a maid named Miss Bessie Green. And they beat her almost to death."

She looked at me in astonishment. "I heard about Bessie Green in church. Our pastor asked us to pray for her. But I had no idea that it was your lady who hurt her. I don't want you nowhere near that place. You go on out to Vegas with Mandy's boys. I know that you'll be a good girl. Do you have any idea who you're going to be living with?"

"I'm sure that I can stay with Ben or Alice one. And Bertha would even let me stay with them for a while, if push came to shove."

I stood up and hugged her. "Thanks, Mama. I can't be here tomorrow morning because she'll send Toby to get me again. So, I want to go to Madison and see Gloria. I can stay out there until you all come for Miss Esther's funeral on Monday. Then I'll come back with you-all."

"Okay. Bailey can take you out there after supper."

We went back into the kitchen and finished our supper. Granddaddy was already through and was drinking a cup of coffee. After we finished, I washed the dishes and Mama dried them. Granddaddy sat there and listened to us talk. I was telling them about things that went on around the diner. I told them not to get angry with Toby if he came after me, because it wasn't his fault.

After we finished cleaning, I went to my room and got ready to go. I kissed Mama good-bye and Granddaddy drove me to Madison. We didn't talk at all on our way to Madison. I guess we both had a lot on our minds. We both were about to go through a major change in our lives. When we got to Madison, he sat and ate a dish of ice cream Gloria had given him. Before he left, he gave me a kiss on the forehead and I told him that I would see him on Monday.

Gloria was doing a lot better for herself. She had rented her a cute little shot-gun house. But, she was just as weird as ever. She still thought that somebody had her "fixed" and it was keeping her from getting a man. There were candles burning everywhere. Even in her clothes closets. She had one for every occasion. And she told me what each one was for. There was one to ward off evil, one to attract the right man, and one for money, to get it and hold onto it. And so forth and so on.

"If I didn't burn this one," she said pointing to the green one, "my pay would slip right through my fingers. And I wouldn't know what I'd done with it."

It would be a fair assumption that you spent it on candles. But what do I know.

Candles were everywhere and there were spares for when the ones that were burning went out. She hummed a tune most of the time when we weren't talking. And she laughed easy about things that weren't funny. I usually just took her behavior for granted. But I was noticing her closely because I was leaving. I was wondering if she might get worse without me around to talk to. Ben was sending her a little money here and there. But that wasn't like having somebody to talk to. She didn't like talking to Mama, because Mama didn't agree with her beliefs. And Aunt Mandy made the mistake of calling her crazy to her face.

I told her that Johnnie, Bertha and Gene were here from Las Vegas. "Johnnie told me to tell you hello. And if he don't get to come by before Monday, he will see you then."

"How long are they going to be here?"

"They're leaving Tuesday. And I'm going back with them."

"You are?" she asked excitedly.

"Yes. I'm going out there to work. But you know you're going to be the only one left here. Do you want us to send for you?"

"No the big cities scare me. I like to hear the roosters crowing and the frogs croaking. But I'm glad to see you going. You can send me something pretty when you get out there."

"You can bank on it."

"And tell Alice to send me something too. She wrote me when she lived with Ben, but I haven't heard from her since."

"I'll tell her to write to you. And I'll write you too."

"I won't be lonesome with all that mail."

I enjoyed being around her because she was so good-hearted. It was a pity that someone so kind lost her mind.

She cleaned house, washed and ironed for two different families. So Saturday I went with her and helped her. On Sunday we attended church together. And on Monday, we attended Miss Esther's funeral. After the funeral, we all met at Miss Esther's house that Bertha grew up in. My grandparents came and brought food. Gloria got a chance to visit with Johnnie, Bertha, and Gene. Johnnie, Gloria, and Ben were close to the same age so we all had a lot of fun together. When the gathering was over, I rode back home with Gloria to get my things and she drove me back to Canton.

I spent most of the night sorting out things and packing. Mama baked a pound cake and fried some chicken for us to take on the road. She told me that Mrs. Grimes didn't send anybody looking for me on Saturday. I was glad that they didn't have to deal with that mess.

On Tuesday morning, Johnnie was at my house at seven o'clock sharp. Mama had gotten up with me at 5:30 a.m. and I was all ready. Johnnie came in to say good-bye to Mama and Granddaddy. He asked me for my luggage and carried them to his car. I followed him out and paid him the twenty-five dollars. Then I ran back up on the porch and hugged and kissed my grandparents again. Mama was holding the sack of food that she had packed for all of us. I took it and climbed into the backseat with Gene. Our grandparents came out to the car to say good-bye to him and Bertha. Gene was barely awake, but I was wide awake and ready to start my journey West.

CHAPTER V

Mossy…

One day during lunch, I was standing against a tree reading when Ruben James walked up to me. He was the captain of the track team and very popular.

"Mossy, do you already have a date for the freshman and sophomore ball?"

"Who wants to know?"

"Maybe I do."

"I know that you're just kidding. But, no I don't have a date."

"Neither do I. So will you do me the honor of going with me?"

I closed my book hard. "Ruben James, who put you up to this?"

Some of the girls had come closer and were looking at us, so I thought that a prank was being played on me.

"Nobody. I've been watching you on a sly for a long time. I'm just not good with words when it comes to females. And that's why I haven't approached you. Now when it comes to the fellows, I can talk up a blue streak. So what do you say? Will you go with me?"

"Okay," I said smiling. "If you really mean it, I'll go with you."

"I really mean it. And thank you."

We stood and talked, and I kept cutting my eyes looking for Dora Mae. But I didn't see her. I wanted her to see that I had somebody to talk to too. When she finally saw me talking to Ruben, I could tell that she was jealous because she just looked at us and rolled her eyes.

After that day, we talked everyday between classes. But in light of my situation, we had a strained relationship. I didn't feel like I was good enough for one of the most popular boys at the school. He would be trying to talk to me and I would be unconsciously walking away. He was constantly saying wait a minute, I'm not through talking to you. We talked right up to a week before the ball. Then all hell broke loose.

Unbeknownst to me, he had planned to come to my house the following Sunday. He had told some of his teammates that he was going to surprise me by coming and asking my parents for permission to walk me to church. He had even bragged to them about how suave he was going to be, and my parents wouldn't have the heart to turn him down. I had made the mistake of telling him where I lived during one of our conversations. But when he got there that Sunday, Mama and I had already left for church, so Daddy answered the door when he knocked.

"Good morning Mr. Lewis, Sir," Ruben said.

But Mr. Lewis didn't answer him. Ruben scratched his head and said, "Mr. Lewis, my name is Ruben James. And I go to school with your daughter Mossy. I came by to ask your permission to walk her to church."

Mr. Lewis opened the screen door. "Come on in, I'll get Mossy."

"Thank you Sir," Ruben said and stepped inside.

Mr. Lewis showed him to a chair. "Have a seat. I'll be right back with Mossy."

Ruben sat down and listened for Mr. Lewis to call Mossy. When he didn't hear anything, he figured that Mr. Lewis had to go out in the back to get her, and that her Mama was probably out there with her.

"This is a nice house."

But the stillness bothered him. It was down right spooky. There were some portraits on the mantle and he wanted to walk over and look at them, but he was too afraid to move.

"What's keeping Mr. Lewis so long?"

He hoped that he hadn't come at a bad time. Mr. Lewis was not a talkative man, and there was something about his demeanor that was troubling. Now that he thought about it he could feel the hair rise on the back of his neck. He wished that he had looked at the clock when he first sat down. But even though he hadn't, he knew that he had been sitting there at least eight to ten minutes. Not that he was impatient. It was just that the whole thing felt strange. He looked at the front door.

I could just leave. I'll tell Mossy since she took so long; I thought that she didn't want to see me. Because, that's probably what it is, and her daddy just isn't having any luck at talking her into it. Yes, I'll just leave.

He stood up. But just as he stood up, he saw Mr. Lewis, and he was coming toward him with a double barrel shotgun.

Ruben started to run, but Mr. Lewis hollered, "Halt! Don't you run from me boy," he said in a calm voice. "I don't wanna have to drop you. I just wanna talk to you."

He held up both hands, so that the old man wouldn't consider him a threat, and turned around slowly to face him. The old man walked up to him and put the barrel of the gun under his chin.

"Now looka here boy. Mossy is not taking company. She's too young. But even when she's old enough, I don't want her with the likes of you. I want you to stay away from my daughter. And keep your mouth shut about this. If you do like I tell you, I'll let you live. Do you understand me?"

"Yes Sir," he muttered without moving his mouth. He wanted to lie and say that was not his intentions. He was going to tell him, "Your daughter and I are just friends and schoolmates, but he was afraid to move even his mouth.

Mr. Lewis took the gun from under his chin. "Now git!" He almost tore the screen off the door getting out of there. He got off the porch so fast that he didn't remember using the steps. He hit the ground running and didn't stop until he was off their property and on the main road.

Daddy didn't even mention that Ruben had been to our house. But I noticed an abrupt change in Ruben at school the next day. I wore my new dress that Aunt Florence had just finished, and I was anxious for him to see me wearing it. But at lunch time when I started toward him, he walked the other way. I didn't pursue him because I knew that he'd seen me.

It was nice while it lasted. But now he has gotten cold feet. Oh well, I didn't want to attend that stupid ball anyway. I hate every phony one of them. Ruben and Dora Mae have taught me that they can't be trusted, so from now on, I'll just keep to myself.

But the next day, while we were changing classes, I saw Ruben looking at me. I walked up and said, "Hi Ruben."

"Just stay away from me," he sneered.

What made it worst was that old nosy Vera heard him. "What was that all about? I thought that you two were getting chummy."

"Mind your own business for a change!" I yelled and walked away.

The next time that I was near Ruben, I didn't even look his way. The Thursday before the ball, I was leaning against a tree reading. Billy Duncan walked up to me and said, "Hi."

I knew that he and Ruben were friends and teammates. *Here I go again.*

"What in the heck do you want?"

"Don't be cruel. I suppose that you won't be coming to the ball."

"So what if I don't? What do you care?"

"I can see where you got your temper from. Your daddy is one bad dude. I sure wish that I had his fireworks. But you may end up being an old maid."

"What are you talking about?"

"I'm not at liberty to say."

He laughed and started to walk away. But I grabbed his arm.

"Billy, please tell me what you're talking about. What did my Daddy say to you?"

"He didn't say anything to me. The question should be, 'What did he say and do to Ruben?'"

"Ruben don't know my Daddy."

"Oh yes he does. I'm not supposed to say anything, but he was at your house Sunday."

I felt a lump in my throat the size of a cannonball. I thought that I was going to choke, but I managed to get out, "Did he tell you what happened?"

"Come on. I'll tell you what he told me. But you have to promise me that you won't tell a soul, or Ruben could get hurt. The only reason that I'm telling you this is so you won't think hard of Ruben. Because, he likes you and so do some of the rest of us."

I promised him that I wouldn't tell and we started walking away from the other students. I didn't ask what he meant about some other people that liked me; my mind was focused on the matter at hand.

We walked and he told me everything that Ruben had told him. When we reached the edge of the school yard, we started walking back.

"Tell Ruben that I'm sorry."

"I can't. I was not supposed to tell you. And you can't apologize to him either. Just leave it alone. He's not blaming you and it will all come out in the wash."

"Thank you for telling me Billy. I promise you that it won't go any farther."

Back in class, the teacher asked me a question and I said that I didn't know. I did know the answer, but I was afraid to say more than a few words, for fear that I would burst out crying. I felt devoid of hope. My Daddy had ruined my life in every way. There were only two things left to do, because after last Sunday's sermon, I had ruled out killing him. My choices now were to run away or kill myself. On my way home, I'd have to decide which one to do.

When the bell rang, I was the first one out of my seat. On my way home, my heart felt heavy. I had to breathe hard through my mouth to keep my heart from bursting. I was overwhelmed by despair. If I ran away, where could I go? I didn't have a single friend. And Ellen had made it plain that I couldn't stay with her. If she knew what was happening to me, she'd do something about it. I knew she would. But if I told her, Daddy would kill us both. He had said that he would rather be dead than to go to the pen again. Now I was down to one choice. And that was to kill myself. But how was I going to do it, if I was afraid of blood? Miss Mozell had poisoned herself to death when her cancer got so bad that she couldn't stand it. She'd made herself some tea with a poisonous herb. But I couldn't remember the name of the herb. I wanted to die a painless death, if there was any such thing.

All at once, something Aunt Florence always said echoed in my head. And then, I knew exactly what I was going to do. Almost every time she took a dip of snuff, she would say this stuff is going to kill me yet. So I figured that if I took enough at one time, it would kill me right away. Now that I had it all figured out, I hastened my steps. When I got home, I did my chores so Mama wouldn't call me or look for me until supper was ready. And by that time, I'd be eating supper with Saint Peter. I fed Betsy and Red last and whispered good-bye to them. Then I went into the house and stole a bottle of Daddy's snuff. I had heard him and Aunt Florence talking about notches, so I knew that his snuff was stronger than hers. I figured it was subject to work faster.

I filled a mason jar with water and took the snuff and the water to my room. I closed my door and set the snuff and water on my bureau. I stood there looking at it and trying to build up my nerve. Something in my head said, *Do it. This is your only way out.*

I picked up the snuff and held my nose. I poured a large amount into my mouth. And then I drank some water behind it and I lay down and closed my eyes. *Pretty soon, it will be all over.*

It seemed like in less than a minute, my stomach started heaving. And I barely made it to the bathroom. When I finished throwing up, I sat on the floor by the toilet. When I gained my repose, I staggered back to my room and fell across my bed.

Mama came to my door. "What's wrong?"

"Nothing," I said in a drowsed voice.

"I heard you throwing up."

"It was just something I ate at school."

"I'll make you some tea," she said and left.

That was the one time that I was glad that she was so unobservant. The snuff bottle was sitting right there on my bureau and she hadn't noticed it. I pulled myself up and pushed the jar under my bed. When she returned with the tea, I told her to set it on my nightstand. All the snuff had done was made me sick and light-headed. And I wished that I could have died.

I didn't go to school that Friday. I didn't want anybody asking me about the ball. Mama didn't go to work either. Aunt Florence came over and they both waited on me hand and foot. I stayed in the bed until the afternoon.

When I went back to school on Monday, I asked Vera if Ruben had gone to the ball.

"Yes. And he came stag. Don't that make you feel good?"

"Then who did he dance with?"

"I only saw him dance a couple of times. But I don't remember who he danced with."

Maybe he does like me. But a lot of good it's going to do me. He's afraid of being around me.

I don't know why, but for some reason, just knowing that a nice boy liked me helped to sustain me. The ball had come and gone and my darkest cloud had passed over. I no longer had suicidal tendencies. I was looking ahead to commencement day. And then I would take the first thing smoking on wheels out of Marlin.

My last three years of school were much better than the previous ones. My grades were coming back up and I was sure that I was going to graduate. I had even begun to feel a little better about myself. Part of that was due to Aunt Florence always telling me how pretty I was. And Daddy stopped raping me altogether. Lately, he was down more than he was up. He hardly ever left the house anymore. And he acted like he couldn't stand me, which was fine by me. Because, I couldn't stand him either. I knew that it was because he didn't have that control over me any longer. He had lost his sexual drive.

Every once in a while, Mama and I would get into it and he would tell her to send me to the reform school. I would yell, "Yes, go ahead and send me. Any place is better than this hell hole."

I would say it every time, until I asked Aunt Florence, "What is a reform school?"

"It's a jail for bad girls and boys. You don't want to go there."

So I stopped yelling at Mama to go ahead and send me. Until Aunt Florence had set me straight, I thought that a reform school was an institution for children without parents.

Nobody else wanted them, so the reform school housed and educated them. I thought since they didn't have a home and parents, they wouldn't be as snooty as the children at my school, so I would be able to find a best friend easily. Plus, I wouldn't always have to be worried about Daddy getting well and raping me again. But as time went by, I started to relax. He had even stopped looking at me in that lustful way. Finally home was better than being at reform school.

From time to time, I thought about what Billy told me about some of the rest of them that liked me too. When I reached the eleventh grade, I began to wish that one of them would come forth because I was going to need a date for the Junior and Senior Proms. But when prom night came, nobody had asked, so I stayed home. Even Dora Mae had a date. Of course I wouldn't have gone to a dog fight with her date. He had the bumpiest face I'd ever seen. I didn't even like him to sit near me in the lunch hall.

Ruben and Billy had graduated that year and I never saw Ruben again. I heard that he went away to college on a scholarship. I saw Billy in town sometimes, and Mama and I visited his church. But he never said more than hi to me. He never did tell me who my secret admirer was, and I was too bashful to ask him. I figured that Ruben and he must have put the word out about me, because nobody asked to take me to my Senior Prom either.

Some of the girls had told me, "It is an event that you don't want to miss. It is the most memorable night of your life." Ellen had bought my dress in Dallas. It was a beautiful pink chiffon dress. It would have probably been the prettiest dress at the prom. I was tempted to go alone, but that evening I decided that staying home was better than being a wallflower. So I stayed home and cried.

The next big event was Commencement Day. Ellen came home and brought me some presents. Mama, Aunt Florence and members from our church gave me presents too. Daddy didn't attend my graduation, but I couldn't care less. When

Ellen got ready to go back home, I asked, "Can I go back with you?"

"I will talk it over with Mama. And I'll take you back for the summer the next time I come, if Daddy keeps doing as well as he is doing."

But I had my mind made up that I was leaving. No matter what condition Daddy was in. And if Ellen wouldn't let me live with her, I would go West to live with Sarah or Rachel, preferably Sarah. Rachel was the oldest, but she liked to tease too much. She got on my nerves.

Monday after graduation, I set my alarm clock to get up with Mama. When my alarm went off, she was already stirring. I jumped up, washed up, got dressed and went out to the kitchen. Mama was finishing her coffee.

"Why are you up with the roosters?"

"I want to go into town with you and help you. I want to work with you and make some money. I'm planning to move to Dallas with Ellen, just as soon as I have enough money. I'll work for ten dollars a week."

She looked up at me. "Did Ellen ask you to come to Dallas?"

"No Ma'am. I asked her. She said that she was going to ask you if I could spend the summer with her. But I want to move there for good."

"Have you lost you mind? You're only seventeen. You're not leaving here yet. And Ellen is not settled enough to look out for you."

"I can look after myself. I'll be eighteen in August. That's just two months away."

"It's out of the question."

She got up and put her cup and saucer in the sink. "I'll let you make some money. But, I want you to go to college, so when I'm dead and gone, you can provide for yourself."

"Yes Ma'am."

I figured that there was no need to provoke her and make her change her mind about letting me make the money.

Because, once I had the money, I could do with it as I pleased.

"What do you want me to do first?"

I didn't relish the idea of peddling. I didn't want my schoolmates to see me. But it was the only way that I knew how to make some fast money. Then I would be gone and they'd never see them again anyway.

"You can start with milking the cows, gathering the eggs and feeding the animals. Then you can clean out that henhouse."

I frowned because I still dreaded going in there.

"After that, you can clean up around here. And that's all that I can think of right now."

"And you're going to pay me ten dollars every Friday?"

"Yes. If you stay on the job and I don't have to keep getting on you."

"You won't."

"I left some biscuits and ham in the warmer."

"Yes Ma'am. Do you need me to help you load the truck?"

"It's already loaded. I got up real early. I just couldn't sleep for some reason."

"I'll have everything done when you get back."

The thought of that ten dollars a week put pep in my steps. I was going to leave as soon as I made forty dollars, because with the thirty that I had gotten for graduation, that would give me seventy. And that would be enough to help Ellen out with rent and food until I found work. I thought about eating breakfast while the biscuits were still warm, but I consulted with my stomach, and it was still asleep. So I grabbed the milk pail and went out and milked the cows.

When I got back in the kitchen, Daddy was up and sitting at the table eating.

"Good morning," I said, without looking at him.

He might have spoke, I can't be sure, but I didn't hear him. I walked over to the counter and sat the milk pail down.

Then I started washing my hands in the kitchen sink. He got up from the table and walked up behind me. He put his arms around my waist.

"I didn't congratulate you for finishing up. So, I want to do it now."

"Thank you Daddy," I said and tried to walk away.

"Wait a minute," he said and held me tighter. "I'm going to get you something real nice for finishing up. But one kindness deserves another."

He was talking directly into my ear because I'd grown almost as tall as him. "Let me go!" I said in an angry voice. "I don't need another present, I have enough."

He held on as tight as he could and said, "Let me make you feel good. I want to show you what I can do with my tongue."

I thought about elbowing him to make him turn me aloose. But, he was still stronger than me and may hurt me. So I thought that I better sweet talk him so I could get the upper hand.

"You never did that. Do you want to go to my room?"

"You mean it?" he asked, still holding on to me.

"Yes Sir."

He turned me aloose and I started down the hall. As soon as I was out of his reach, I ran. I ran into their bedroom and grabbed his shotgun out of the closet. By then, he had made it to their bedroom door. He stood there stunned, looking at his gun and then at me. I cocked the gun.

"You better not come any closer."

"Have you gone crazy? You give me my gun right now or I'll go call the law."

"You're the one who's crazy!" I snapped. "And if you move one peg toward me, you're dead!"

We stood there for a few seconds and then I yelled, "Backup, and let me out of here."

I was going to leave the house and take the gun with me. But he backed away and then turned and rushed to the back door.

"Gal, you've lost your damn mind," he yelled as he rushed out of the back door. "And I'm going into town and get the law to get you out of my house."

I ran to the back door and locked it behind him. Then I checked the front door to make sure that it was locked. I didn't want him to sneak up on me while I was getting some of my things together. I held on to his shotgun and watched from the kitchen window until I saw him leave on his horse. Then I put the shotgun back in their bedroom closet and ran to my bedroom and started packing. I didn't have time to look for Mama's suitcase, so I grabbed the pillowcase off my pillow and started cramming as much stuff as I could get into it. I packed mostly underwear and summer clothes. When it was full, I sat it down by my bedroom door and stood there for a while looking about my bedroom.

I started remembering how happy I was to have a room by myself after Ellen, who is eleven years older, left home. To make it feel like my own, Mama had bought me a pink bedspread and pink curtains to match. I had so many pretty things that I had collected over the years. I hated to leave them behind, but the pillowcase was already overstuffed. And my trunk was out of the question. I wouldn't be able to carry it. I thought maybe I could send Ellen back for some more of my things. But right now, I had to hurry and get on the road before Daddy got back with the law. Although we lived out in the rural, from the small town of Marlin, Texas, it wouldn't take him long to get back. But I wasn't going to be here to get arrested for attempted murder.

I couldn't leave without saying farewell to my dogs, and they also needed to be fed. I sat my things down by the front door and went to the kitchen to feed them. I took a dishpan, put the skillet of cornbread that I'd made for them in it and poured all of the fresh milk that was in the pail on the bread.

Then I sat it on the back porch for them. I gave them each a hug and told them so long. As I started to leave the house, I thought about the thirty dollars that I had of my own money. That wasn't going to go far. I needed that forty dollars that I'd planned to make, so I would just have to borrow it from Mama. I went into their bedroom and found the key to her chifforobe. I opened it and took forty dollars from her stash. I put the rest back and locked the door.

I said to myself, "I'll pay her back as soon as I find work." And then I thought, *Maybe I will and maybe I won't, because she is part to blame for what happened to me. She let it happen. Mothers are supposed to sense when something is wrong with their children, especially for that many years. But she had continued to ignore it, so she owes me.*

Ellen's telephone number was pinned on the wall in her room so I copied it down. I put the money and telephone number in my purse. I got my clothes and went out and locked the front door. I put the key in the cache and left.

I hadn't been on the road no time before a truck pulled up beside me and stopped. I looked up and saw that it was Billy Duncan and thought, *Oh, no!*

I was hoping that I wouldn't run into anybody that I knew. I felt embarrassed and tried to play it off. I sat my things on the ground. "Hi Billy, whose truck did you steal?"

He turned his engine off and got out. "It's mine," he said smiling and walking toward me. "I'm buying it off my Daddy because I need transportation to find work. I'm not working in the fields no more. Where are you going?"

"Give me a lift and I'll tell you"

"Okay," he said and took my pillowcase and put it in the back of his truck. We got into the cab and he pulled off. "Where are you going?" he asked again.

"I'm going to Dallas to live with Ellen."

"So why are you walking?"

"My parents don't want me to leave. So I'm running away while they're gone. Will you help me? I have the money to pay you."

"You don't have to pay me. Where do you want me to take you?"

"Well, I would like to go to Waco. Because I don't know if my parents are in Marlin or Lott. So, I would like to bypass both and catch the bus in Waco."

"Then let's go," he said and sped up.

"I hope that I don't get shot over this."

"Don't be silly. Who's going to know?"

"If I get this gig at the sawmill, I'll save some money and move to Dallas too. Maybe then we can get together."

I was shocked to hear that. I looked at him and asked "What?"

"You heard me. I've been liking you for a long time. But I couldn't do anything about it because Ruben liked you. He was my friend and I didn't want to hurt him. Did you hear that he got a scholarship?"

"Yes, I heard about it. I'm happy for him. Did he tell anybody else what my daddy done besides you?"

He thought for a while and then answered, "Yes he did. I tried to get him not to do it, but he was a sore loser. If he couldn't have you, he didn't want anybody else to have you either."

"That explains why nobody asked to take me to the prom. I'll never forgive Ruben for that."

"But part of it was because he didn't want anybody to get shot."

"I don't want to talk about it anymore!" I said sharply. "You're just taking up for him. He should have minded his own business."

We covered a number of subjects before we reached Waco. When we got there, he parked and got out with me. He carried my pillowcase into the bus station, and I bought a ticket for Dallas. He bought us each a banana split and stayed with me until the bus came. We exchanged addresses and I promised to write.

He told me, “I’m so glad that I happened to come along when I did. What kind of work are you planning to look for in Dallas?”

“I’m going to work in a department store. Ellen already works there and I’m sure that she can get me on.”

When they announced my bus over the loud speaker, he stood in line with me. After I gave the driver my ticket, Billy asked, “Can I carry her things on for her?”

The driver looked at the overstuffed pillowcase and said, “Go ahead.”

Billy tried to tie the top of the pillowcase, but it was too full. So I told him, “Just sit it on the seat beside me.”

He kissed me on the forehead and said, “I’ll write to you.

He left the bus and waited outside until the bus pulled away. Tears fell from my eyes as I waved to him, but I quickly wiped them away and let out a sigh. I was finally free of my daddy.

CHAPTER VI

Alice…

Blanche and Jean dressed up sexy and went out almost every night. And two weeks later, Blanche took me to get my false I.D. like she had promised. It only cost me three dollars. The guy said that he would make me a fake birth certificate for five dollars. They took me out that night, after I got my I.D. We went to a nightclub on the Set. I had my first cocktail, vodka and milk over ice. Blanche ordered it for me. She called it a white cow. I didn't like it at first, but I soon acquired a taste for it. We sat there drinking and listening to the band. There was gonna be a talent show later on that was supposed to be good. Jean had a small bottle of liquor in her purse, and she was using it to make her cocktails stronger. When we were ordering our second round, she was ordering her third. And she was trying to get the waitress's attention to order a fourth round when Jeff walked in.

I saw him when he first walked through the curtain. He stood against the wall looking around for Jean. I didn't tell her that he was there. I was thinking about excusing myself to go to the restroom so I could pass him and speak to him. But before I got up the nerve, he'd spotted us. He walked over to the table and whispered to Jean. And she got up and followed him outside of the club. They exited from a side door. She came back inside alone. She came over to the table and whispered in Blanche's ear. Blanche leaned over said to me, "Let's go." The three of us walked out together.

"I thought that we were gonna see the talent show," I said.

"We'll bring you back next week," Blanche said. "But right now, we have got to take care of some business on the Strip."

On our way to Jean's car, she told me, "We don't have time to drop you off at home. So, I want you to follow our lead and keep quiet."

Blanche asked Jean if she wanted her to drive, but Jean said that she was okay. We got in Jean's Ford and started to the Strip. Jean was wavering all across the road. And she even ran a stop sign.

Blanche was constantly yelling, "Girl, watch what you're doing."

Jean kept saying, "I've got it under control."

When she tried to park on the Strip, she side-swiped a parked car, and asked Blanche, "Why didn't you tell me that I was that close to that car?"

"I thought that you had it under control," Blanche said snidely.

She backed up and got out of that space and drove a ways down the row of parked cars. When she tried to park again, she side-swiped another car. Blanche ended up parking the car after all.

"You're not getting these keys back tonight," Blanche told her. "I'm not going to keep quiet and let you kill me."

"I'll be all right, as soon as I get some air."

We got out of the car and went into the hotel where Jeff worked. We found the elevators and stood there waiting for an available one. Jean turned to Blanche and asked, "What floor is it?"

"Hell, I don't know. He didn't tell me, he told you."

"But I thought that I told you at the club."

"If you did, I didn't catch it over all that noise."

"I'm sure that the room number is sixteen. I'm just kinda fuzzy about the floor."

"Well, why don't we find a telephone and have Jeff paged at the club."

An elevator came but we didn't catch it because Jean wasn't sure of where we were going. "Let's go call him," Blanche urged.

"No. I know Jeff. He'll get mad and call me stupid. I'm sure now that it was room 316."

"Then let's go."

I was still wondering what was going on. We caught the next elevator and got off on the third floor. We found room 316 and Jean took out a key and unlocked the door. The three of us went into the room and locked the door behind us. Blanche and Jean started searching the room. They looked in suitcases, the closet, dresser drawers and every place else. They tore that room apart in a matter of seconds. By this time, I knew that it was money that they were after. So I just stood near the door to listen out for them. I was so scared that I was shaking. The only money that was found was a cup of quarters on the dresser. But they didn't want them.

"Maybe this is the wrong room," Jean said. "Because, Jeff said that the money would be visible."

"Then let's get the hell out of here!" Blanche yelled heading towards the door.

But just then, we heard people coming. They were laughing and talking. We huddled at the door waiting for them to pass. But they stopped in the front of room 316. We all ran to the window and Jean opened it and jumped out. Blanche jumped right behind her. I could hear the key in the lock as I stood there waiting to jump. I landed on top of Jean and Blanche. I heard them both cry out in agony. My forehead hit the ground and I felt like my head had exploded. My elbow hit the ground also, but my head was the only pain that I felt. But I still managed to get to my feet and so did Blanche.

I felt blood running down my face and I wiped my face with my torn dress. I looked up at the window that we had jumped from but I didn't see anybody. I was staggering away holding my head, when I heard Blanche calling me. My ears were ringing and her voice sounded far away. But she was right behind me. She was tugging at Jean, trying to get her to her feet. And she was asking me to help her. Jean was in excruciating pain. When Blanche asked her if she could walk, she cried out that her legs were broken, so we picked her up together and started to the car with her. A black hotel employee walked up and asked us what was wrong and if we needed some help?

"No Sir, thank you," Blanche said. "Our friend is just a little drunk."

We wanted him to go on about his business, but he stood there watching us. He knew that Blanche was lying, because blacks weren't allowed to drink and socialize at a bar or lounge on the Strip. Besides, we were ragged and bleeding like hogs. We got Jean in the back seat of her car and we got in and drove away.

We were safe from being arrested, but there was still the matter of getting Jean some medical help fast. She was on the back seat moaning and groaning something awful.

Please take me to a hospital."

"Just hold on," Blanche told her. "I need some help with this. We're going to the Westside to get Rooster. He'll know what to do."

"Please hurry," Jean moaned. "I can't stand this pain."

"Just hold on," Blanche said. "We're going to get you to a hospital. How is your head?"

"It hurts. But, I'll be all right. I don't wanna go to no hospital."

I had held my dress against my forehead and it had slacked up bleeding. Blanche drove to Rooster's apartment and went in and told him what had happened. He let Blanche drive his car to bring the two of us home and he drove Jean to the hospital in her car. When we got home and I got cleaned up, I saw that my forehead had just a small cut, but it was swollen real bad. My knees and elbow were skinned up real bad too. Blanche's knees and elbow were also skinned up, but she was more concerned about ruining her nice clothes. Jean was hurt the worst because Blanche and I both landed on her. She was admitted to the hospital with two broken legs. She told the doctors that she got drunk and fell from a second floor balcony onto the concrete.

Rooster came to see about us after he left the hospital. Shortly after he got there, Jeff drove up. He saw Jean's car and thought that she was back from her mission. He knocked on the door and Rooster let him in. He walked in smiling from ear to ear.

"Jeff, have a seat," Blanche said.

"I just need to see Jean. I can't stay. Is she back there?" he asked pointing to her room.

"No. She's in the hospital."

"Hospital? What is wrong with her?"

"We had to jump from a third floor window and she broke both of her legs. Rooster just got back from the hospital."

"Man, will you please tell me what's going on?" he asked Rooster.

"Let Blanche tell you man, because I wasn't there. They came and got me out of bed to drive Jean to the hospital."

Jeff looked over at Blanche and she asked him, "Did you know how drunk Jean was when you sent her on that job?"

"She seemed a little high but not drunk."

"She was drunk. At first, I thought that she was just nervous about the job. But if I had known that her head was that bad, I wouldn't have gone with her. We're lucky to be alive."

"What is this about some third floor window?"

"She couldn't remember what floor we were supposed to go to. I told her to call you at the club, but then she said that she remembered that it was room 316. Was that where you sent her?"

"Hell no!" Jeff exclaimed. "It was room 615."

"Well she took us in room 316 and the people were coming. And the window was the only way out because I wasn't going to jail, not tonight. We all got hurt, but her injuries were the worst. She broke both legs and Alice and I had to carry her."

"I'm hearing this shit, but I don't believe it. That stupid bitch should have broke her Got Damn neck! I repeated myself at least three times and she still fucked up.

Those words should have given me a clue to the type of person he was, but I wasn't thinking straight. To me it meant that he didn't really love her, and that I had a chance with him. I was in love and couldn't see the forest for the trees. I was the only one who laughed when he made that comment. I was trying to show my approval of him. But he didn't even notice me. All he was thinking about was that the deal fell through. Blanche kept talking and she told him again to have a seat.

"No, I've got to go," he said, and walked out of the door.

Blanche looked at me. "Alice, I'm sorry that you got involved in this mess, and on your first night out too."

"It's okay. I survived it and that's all that counts. It wasn't your fault, but I could use some aspirins."

"They're in the medicine cabinet. And you can sleep in Jean's room for the time being. She won't be using it for a while."

"Thanks. Then I'll turn in now."

I took three aspirins and eased into bed. That fall had begun to take its toll on me. I was sore all over. Rooster spent the night with Blanche, and he checked on me the next morning before he left. He was a nice guy. He even looked a little better to me.

Blanche didn't go to work the next day. She was too sore. Jeff came back that evening and told Blanche about the project that he had sent them on. As it turned out, there was a high-roller from Texas occupying room 615 at the hotel where we went. He had heard about the man from Leonard, a men's room attendant. The gentleman had asked Leonard to fix him up with a nice clean black woman, for a price of course. He gave Leonard his room number and told him where he could be reached. He was going to be playing in a Baccarat Tournament that night. Leonard turned the job of finding the woman over to Jeff, who was in that business and they planned to split the fee. But Jeff got other ideas after talking to the maid that had cleaned the room. In conversation, she told him how careless the occupant was with his money. 'There's large bills lying everywhere,' she told Jeff. 'But, I'm not about to touch one red cent and get fired.' Jeff found out what time the evening Baccarat Tournament would be in session and then flirted with a housekeeper who was sweet on him and stole a pass key. He had come by the apartment looking for Jean and Blanche but we had already left for the club. If things had gone down the way they were planned, this man would have been robbed while he was playing Baccarat. By the time Jeff found us in the nightclub, time was of an essence. And that's how I became involved.

He addressed me for the first time. "I'm sorry that you got caught up in this mess."

"Oh, it's okay. Really it is."

"We spoiled your first night out. But maybe I can make it up to you."

Blanche looked at him and then at me.

"I'll bring you all some bar-be-cue ribs by since you all are going to be shut in for a while."

Then he asked Blanche, "When are you returning to work?"

"I'm taking tomorrow off and then the next two days are my off days."

"Well, I'll bring you all that bar-be-cue. I'll see you later." He got up and left.

As soon as he was out of the door, Blanche told me, "I hope you don't get your mouth tuned up for bar-be-cue, because you'll never get it if he has to buy it for you."

"Why? Is he stingy?"

"How many times do I have to tell you about that dude? If he didn't want to buy Jean a hamburger, why do you think that he's going to spend money on bar-be-cue for us? He won't buy himself more than a bowl of soup. He puts every dollar that he can rack and scrape on those gambling tables."

"Oh, I forgot."

I was trying not to give myself away, but there was nothing that she could say that would change my mind about Jeff. Nobody that looked that good could be as bad as she claimed.

She's just jealous that her old man Rooster is as ugly as home-made sin.

I was convinced that all Jeff needed was a good woman to make him mend his ways. And I was just the woman that could do it.

We didn't leave the apartment for the next three days. Rooster brought us food. Blanche was Rooster's weakness. He loved her regardless of what she did. And like Blanche said, that bar-be-cue never made it there. During the time that we were housebound, I learned a great deal about my two roommates. Blanche talked about herself and Jean, but everything that I told her about my childhood was a lie. Whenever the subject of my mother and father came up, I quickly changed the subject. I told the same lies over and over. I had begun to believe them myself. I told Blanche that Ben was my half brother, because I didn't know how much she already knew about him.

Blanche called the hospital every day to inquire about Jean and they let her speak to her a couple of times. When we got better, Rooster took us up to the hospital to see Jean. He waited outside while we went in. Jean told us that Jeff had not called or come to see her.

"I'm going to quit his ass when I get out of here."

That was music to my ears. Blanche told Jean what Jeff had told her about that job.

"Fuck him!" Jean shouted. "Why didn't he steal the money his damn self. I don't want to hear any more. Jeff and I are history, I mean it."

A little nosy-ass nurse's aid came in and told us that we had to leave. "You're upsetting my patient."

"It's okay," Jean told her. "I want them to stay. Visiting hours are not over yet."

They stopped talking until the nurse's aid left. "I want you to do something for me," Jean said to Blanche.

"What is it?"

"I want you to come back tomorrow and bring me a bottle. I'm going to go crazy without something to drink."

"I can't do that. Alcohol will make it harder for you to heal."

"I don't want to hear that shit," Jean sneered. "I need a drink. And if you won't get it for me, there ain't no need for you all to come back."

"If that's what you want." Blanche turned to me and said, "Let's go. I'll see you Jean." And we left.

When we were out of the room, I said "You have so much patience with her. Why?"

"Because she's my friend. And she has always stood by me. Shortly after we met in a nightclub, she moved in with me. We were sitting at the bar talking and she mentioned that she was looking for a place to stay. I needed a roommate, so I could have some extra change in my pocket. So we got to talking and she moved in. She may have saved my life one night. Or at least saved me from becoming a freak."

"What happened?"

"I got jumped by two over-the-hill hookers. I was about to go through the side door of the club and one of them grabbed me by my hair and lead me into the alley. They both pulled out a knife and told me that they were going to cut me up. One of them said that I was screwing her man. I didn't even know the person's name that she called. One of them was on each side of me playing in my face with their knives and calling me every dirty name in the book. Some girl ran inside and got Jean and she ran out there and pulled her pistol. Let me tell you, those bitches outran their shadows."

"Do you think that she would have shot them?"

"Hell yes! If you make Jean mad enough, she'll shoot your ass. She's okay, and she makes a good friend if you don't try to fuck over her."

"Then why does she let Jeff treat her so bad?"

"There's a difference. Any woman will take more shit from her man than she will from another woman."

When we got out to the waiting room, Rooster asked about Jean and Blanche told him that she was being a bitch.

"She wants me to sneak her a bottle in here. But I'm not going to do it. She'll get drunk and curse out the doctors and nurses. And they may give her the Black Bottle."

Rooster took us out to eat and then home.

The next day Blanche went back to work. Jeff came by around ten o'clock a.m. and I got butterflies in my stomach when I looked out of the curtains and saw him. I was still in my pajamas, so I grabbed my housecoat, washed my face and combed my hair before opening the door.

"How are you?" he asked as he walked in.

"Fine thank you," I said smiling.

"I was about to leave. I thought that you wasn't going to let me in. I saw you look out of the curtain."

"I wasn't dressed. And I was just trying to get presentable. But if you're looking for Blanche, she went back to work today."

"I'm not here to see Blanche," he said as he walked pass me and sat on the couch.

"Then Jean is still in the hospital."

"I'm not here to see her either."

"Then would you like a glass of water?"

"I would rather a beer. But if you don't have beer, I'll take the water."

"The beer belongs to Blanche, so I better not bother it."

I brought him a glass of water and sat down on the end of the couch.

"You didn't ask me why I'm here."

"I figured that you would tell me."

He laughed and asked, "So how do you like living here?"

"It's okay for the time being. But I'm going to find a job and get my own place."

"They're hiring at all of the laundries."

"Thanks. I'll go and check it out."

I got up and turned on the television and sat back down. I could feel him staring at me but I kept my eyes on the television. He moved over close to me and said, "You know, you're really cute. You're just my type."

"And Jean is not?" I asked, still looking straight ahead.

"She used to be, before she became a lush. That bitch cost me a lot of money the other night. We could have all lined our pockets if she hadn't fucked up. The way I heard it, there was at least a thousand dollars lying around. But I don't want to talk about Jean. I want to talk about us."

"What about us?"

"I want you to be my lady."

"You can't mean that," I said, looking at him. "How would we pull that off?"

"Where there is a will, there is a way. So, are you willing?"

"Yes. But I still don't see how we're gonna do it."

"Just leave it up to me," he said, and he moved in closer and took me in his arms and kissed me.

I kissed him back and tried not to breathe on him. But the kiss was so long, I had to breathe otherwise I would have suffocated. He picked me up and carried me into Jean's room and laid me on her bed. We undressed and made love. I was still a little sore from the fall, but all and all, I gave a pretty good performance. I must have been good because he gave me a hundred dollars. And he told me that he was going to find me a one bedroom apartment so I wouldn't have to be there when Jean got out of the hospital. He took a shower and got dressed.

"I have to go back to work. I'm supposed to be at the doctor's office. But there is no doctor in this world that could have made me feel as good as you just did." We kissed again and he left.

I ran myself a bath and sat in the tub for a long time thinking. I was trying to sift and sort through the events of my life. Things were moving way too fast. But at least I had a man now, somebody in my corner. And he was gonna take care of me. Nobody would give you a hundred dollars if they didn't care something about you. I didn't feel too bad about Jean because they were gonna break up anyway. They both said so. And if I didn't get him, some other woman would.

But I've got to get the hell out of here just the same because Blanche will be just as mad with me as Jean will be. Wouldn't she be surprised if she knew that he gave me this much money. I thought that she was lying on him because she was jealous. And now, I know that was what it was. I hope that I can find a job real soon so I can move. I need to catch a ride out to one of the laundries and apply for a job.

I got out of the tub and got dressed. I straightened up the apartment and walked to the bus stop.

I asked a lady, "Which bus should I catch to get to a laundry?"

"Which one?"

"The closest one I guess. My boyfriend suggested that I go to a laundry to apply for a job."

"I see."

She told me the name of the one that she thought that I'd have the most luck.

"But the buses don't run out that far. So you need to have your boyfriend take you."

"Thank you Ma'am." I started back to the apartment.

I was planning to call Bertha to find out if she could take me. But a young man stopped and asked if I needed a ride.

"Yes thank you," I said and got in his car. I told him the name of the laundry that I was trying to get to. "Can you take me there?"

"Sure, I'll take you. Is that where you work?"

"No. I'm going there to apply for a job."

"My name is Benny Coleman."

"I'm Alice Jones and I'm pleased to meet you."

"I haven't seen you around before."

"Oh, I just moved over on this side of town. I've been living with my brother over on the rich side of town. They have doctors, lawyers and school teachers living over there."

Benny didn't answer. He just looked out of the window on his side.

"How much do I owe you for taking me?"

"Nothing. I'm glad that I'm able to help you. But I'd like to take you to the movie or out to eat sometimes."

"I can't right now because I'm in a relationship. But I don't know if it's gonna work out, so let's stay in touch."

"That sounds good to me. I'll give you my address. I don't have a telephone right now; but I'm going to get one."

I took a pen and piece of paper from my purse and wrote down his address. When we got to the laundry, he asked me if I wanted him to go in with me.

"I would rather go in alone. Just wait for me."

I went to the office and told the man at the desk that I wanted to apply for a job.

"Good," he said smiling. "I have an opening in sorting and one on the mangle."

"What is a mangle?"

"It's those big pressing machines you see out there," he said, pointing to the Mangles. "You feed the damp linen from one side and it comes out on the other. Do you want to try it?"

"Just a little while, I have a ride waiting for me. But, I know that I can do that."

"Then you can just start tomorrow. You'll be working from one o'clock p.m. to nine p.m. And come in a little early, so you can sign some papers."

"Yes Sir, thank you Sir."

I went back out to the car and got in and kissed Benny dead on the mouth. He leaned over for more but I laughed and said, "That was for bringing me. I got the job."

"Congratulations! When do you start?"

"Tomorrow," I said excitedly. "I will be working form one o'clock p.m. to nine p.m. But the only thing is, I've got to find a way to get here."

"You're in luck. I work the graveyard shift, so I can bring you."

"Okay, but I insist on paying you."

"You can pay me by letting me take you out. Whoever your man is, he don't need you like I do."

I just laughed, but I wasn't about to cheat on Jeff. He was much too good of a catch. Benny took me home and I gave him another peck on his lips and got out. I told him that I needed to get there early, and he said that he would pick me up at noon.

I went in the apartment and lit me a cigarette and sat back, smoking and thinking. I was very pleased with myself. Ben hadn't hurt me a bit. I had a job and men were falling out of the sky for me. I decided not to tell Blanche that I was moving until Jeff found the apartment. When she got home, I told her about my job and she was glad, because it meant that I could start paying rent. She asked me if I wanted to go out, but I declined. I had everything that I wanted. There was no need to go out looking. She went out and I stayed home and got ready for work the next day.

Benny took me to work and picked me up three times before I found another ride. I met a girl named Naomi and started paying her to ride with her. But Benny and I remained friends. I just wasn't gonna give him any. It was over a week before I heard from Jeff again. And I began to worry. I was afraid to ask Rooster about him because he would tell Blanche.

When he did show up one morning, he had found me a one bedroom furnished apartment. I told him about my job. I gave him all the credit for telling me where to look. Blanche hit the ceiling when I told her that I was moving.

"When your rent starts kicking you in the ass, don't come crawling back to me!

Benny helped me to move my things. Jeff paid my first month's rent, but he borrowed back fifty dollars of the one hundred that he gave me. And he never mentioned it again. He came to see me every night after I got off from work. And he came in the evening when I was off. He spent the night with me sometimes; but most of the time, we made love and he left. He found out early on that I couldn't cook. The only thing that I cooked for him was hot-links. We had a hot-link sandwich every time he came.

I hadn't been in my apartment a month when Jeff came in one night with a long face.

"What is wrong?"

"Oh you don't want to know."

"Don't tell me, let me guess. You're getting back with Jean."

"No, that's not it."

"Then what is it for crying out loud?"

He sat on the couch with his head in both hands. I sat down beside him and put my arm around him.

"Your problems are my problems. So tell me what is wrong?"

"You wouldn't help me. I know you wouldn't."

"Try me. I'll do anything for you. I love you."

Those words were the biggest mistake of my life. He raised his head and looked elated.

"Do you mean that?"

"Yes, I do. Now tell me what is bothering you."

"I'm about to lose everything. I need some money."

I was too stupid to ask what the "everything" included. I just assumed that he meant his apartment and his car. Maybe he was one payment behind on both.

"I have a little over two hundred dollars saved. You can have it."

"I'll take it. But that is still not enough."

I got up and got my money that I had scrimped and saved for hard times. People had warned me that the work slowed down at the laundry in the winter, when the hotels' guests slowed down. They said that it would be hard to make ends meet, so I was trying to build a little nest egg for winter. I gave Jeff the whole two hundred and twenty dollars that I had saved. He took it and didn't even say thanks. All that he said on the subject was, "You know that I'll always take care of you."

"Can you borrow the rest and I help you to pay it back?"

"You're the only one that I can count on."

"But I don't have anymore."

"You're sitting on a gold mine."

"What are you talking about Jeff?"

I sat on the edge of the couch and faced him.

"I know how you can make twenty-five dollars just to talk to somebody. You don't have to screw this guy. He is just lonely and needs somebody to talk to. At the most, he will ask you to pee on him."

"Are you drunk? Who in the world would pay somebody to pee on them? You're lying. You're trying to trick me."

"This guy is a freak. That's how he gets off."

"Did he tell you that he wanted to be peed on?"

"No. The ladies that he has been with told me that he likes it. If you do this for me, nobody will know but you and me. And when we have enough money saved up, we'll get married and leave Las Vegas."

"Okay, I'll do it for you."

"And you need to have a telephone installed as soon as possible."

"I'll get one when I get paid."

He kissed me and left. He didn't want to make love. I rubbed against him to get him in the mood, but he said that he had to go. I felt proud that I could help him out and I knew that would make him love me more. I was judging him by the way I felt when he gave me the hundred dollars. He came by the next morning before I left for work and gave me this man's address.

"He is expecting you around ten o'clock tonight."

He left me ten dollars so I could take a taxicab. But he didn't even try to give me so much as a kiss or a hug.

The little freak's name was Pete and he lived in a motel near the Strip. When I got there that night, I found out that he didn't only want to be peed on. He also wanted to be whipped. We had a couple of drinks, and he went into the bathroom and came out naked with a wet towel. He told me that he wanted me to pop him on his ass with it and call him "Sweet Daddy" every time I hit him. And when he reached his orgasm, he wanted me to pee on him. I thought that he was going to stand still. I was gonna set his ass on fire. But I had to chase him and when I caught him, that's when I would pop him and call him "Sweet Daddy." He had made a pallet on the floor for the event. I felt like a damn fool, but when he lay out on the pallet, I stood over him and peed on him.

When it was all over, he rolled up the pallet and put it in the bathroom. He asked me to have another drink with him, but I told him that I had to go. I picked up the twenty-five dollars from the dresser and put it in my purse.

"Do you want my phone number?" he asked.

"Why?" I asked, putting on my shoes.

"I would like to see you again sometime."

"Not for twenty-five dollars. That was worth at least fifty dollars."

"If I give you another fifteen dollars, will you take my number and call me?"

"Yes, I'll do it for forty dollars."

So he gave me another fifteen dollars and his number. Then he called me a cab.

When I got home, I ran me a bath and sat in the tub. I was confused. I wanted to believe that if I helped Jeff to make some money, he'd marry me. But I began to wonder if he was gambling the money off like Blanche said. I wanted to ask him to let me hold the money. But I thought, *He might think that I don't trust him. I'm gonna do this for about four months. And if he doesn't say anymore about getting married, I'm gonna quit. And I'm not ever gonna give him all of the money.*

I got out of the tub, dried off and went to bed. I tried not to think about it anymore. The next morning when he came by, I gave him twenty-five dollars and I kept fifteen. We made love and before he left, he told me to have faith in him and we'd soon be man and wife.

That day seemed like a century ago. I had knocked on a lot of hotels, motels, and apartment doors since then. And I'd had some close calls. There were some weird fuckers behind some of those doors. But the money kept me taking the risk. I found out what Blanche meant about my rent kicking my ass. There was not enough work at the laundry in the winter to make ends meet, so I had no choice but to keep shaking my money maker. Jeff and I were more like business partners now than we were lovers. He didn't even pretend that he wanted to marry me anymore. And I was not sure that I wanted to marry him, because I loved him, but I didn't like him.

My cousin Gene told me that he was still fucking around with Jean. Of course he denied it. So far, I'd managed to stay out of Jean's and Blanche's sight. I didn't hang around the Set like they did. I had a few regular customers and sometimes Jeff found a new one for me. I didn't like my life, but I guess that you could just say I was in a rut and I had to live it until I could get out.

CHAPTER VII

Meredith...

When we got to the Westside of Las Vegas, Gene directed Johnnie to Alice's apartment. He pulled up in the front of her apartment and stopped. Gene jumped out and knocked on her door. I got out too and stood beside the car. Alice peeped through her curtain and then snatched her door open. She spoke to Gene and then looked pass him at me and started laughing. She ran to me and hugged me so tight that it hurt. But I didn't let on; I just hugged her back and kissed her on the side of her face. I couldn't believe how much she had aged in just four years. And just like Gene had said, her face wasn't just made up, it was painted. Her make-up was applied in the same fashion as Little Richard's. And her hair was waved up in a pompadour with a red streak in the front. She turned me aloose and said

"My little sister, I'm so glad you're here. Are you gonna stay with me?"

"Sure if you'll have me."

By that time Johnnie and Bertha had gotten out of the car. They spoke and Alice hugged Bertha.

"You-all come on inside and I'll make you-all some Kool-aid."

Gene, Bertha, and I followed her inside. Johnnie went to his car trunk, got my luggage and brought it in.

"Johnnie, thank you for bringing Meredith."

"You're welcome."

I was happy because I had a place to live and I was off the hook. Johnnie didn't know that I had lied to him about Alice expecting me. Everything was going like clockwork. I could tell that Gene and Bertha knew that I was lying when I said it. But I wasn't worried about them telling Johnnie, because they wanted me to come no matter what. Alice gave us all a glass of Kool-aid. When Johnnie, Bertha and Gene finished theirs they got up and left. Gene told me that he would see me the next day. Alice asked me about our grandparents and Gloria. I told her that they were all fine and that she should write to them. I asked her about Ben and his family and she said that they didn't talk.

"Ben thinks that he's too good for his folks," she said. "And you shouldn't get your hopes up."

"I just want to see him. I'm not going to force myself off on him. Do you know how to get in touch with him?"

"His telephone number is in the book."

"He likes Gloria," I said. "He writes and sends her money."

"Well he don't like me, that's all I know."

I wanted to ask her about the gossip that was circulating back home about the reason Ben and she fell out. But Alice never tells the truth about anything, so it would have been a waste of time and might even make her mad.

"You have a real nice place and nice things."

"Thanks."

She started telling me how she acquired some of it, like her television, and how much she paid for them. I was trying to appear interested in what she was saying. But sleep was coming down on me and I could barely keep my eyes open.

After she told me how she came by almost every gadget and what-not, she asked if I was hungry.

"I haven't been to the store. But I have some bread and a couple of dried-up hot links. You can't tell the difference once I boil them, they just plump right back up."

"No thank you. I'm not hungry, but I would like to get some of this grime off me and take a nap."

"Okay. We'll have the hot links and talk when you wake up. I'm supposed to work today, but now I have an excuse to take off. My ride will be here in a little while, but I'm gonna tell her I'm not going."

"Oh no, I don't want you to miss work on my account. Go ahead. I'll take care of your apartment. Just lock me in."

"Don't worry about it. I needed an excuse to rest. I'm tired myself. I didn't get home until five o'clock this morning." She pointed to her bedroom and said, "The bathroom is back there, make yourself at home. I only have one bed so you'll have to sleep with me like we did before I left home. But I'll let you have the bed by yourself for now and I'll take a nap on the couch."

"Okay. I just need a couple of hours, and then I'll get up and keep you company."

I got up and left my purse on the couch. I carried my luggage into the bedroom and took out a change of clothes. Her bathroom was just as nice as Mrs. Grimes's. I ran me a bath and almost fell asleep in the tub. I was just that tired. It was nice not having to heat the water and bathe in a tin tub like I did back home. After a good long bath I got out of the tub, dried off and put my brand new gown on. I got into the bed and just floated off to sleep. There was no doubt in my mind that Las Vegas was the most wonderful place in the world.

I was so exhausted that I slept a lot longer than I had planned. It was first dusk when I was awakened by loud angry voices. The door to the bedroom was closed, but I could still hear Alice arguing with a man. I sat up in bed so I could hear what was being said. The man had come to get some money she owed him from some business deal. But she didn't want to give it to him.

"A deal is a deal!" the man yelled. "And I was counting on that money."

"Why, so you can take it up there on the Set and give it to those damn Chinamen? Because that's what you do with every other dollar you get your hands on."

"What I do with my share is my business!"

"You're right! But I'm tired of putting my life on the line so you can gamble. You've been turning over rocks to find me tricks lately. It's getting too dangerous out there. I'm getting out of the business. And besides, my little sister is here and I don't feel right doing this in front of her."

"Just give me the money Alice, or at least a part of it," he begged.

"No Jeff I can't spare it. I have my little sister to think about. I have two mouths to feed until she finds a job."

"Both of you bitches can go to hell! I'll get your ass for this! Just wait and see if I don't!"

He left and slammed the door as hard as he could. I lay there a little while longer, and then got up and put my housecoat on. I went out into the living room where she was. She was sitting at the dinette table smoking a cigarette, and drinking a beer. She didn't acknowledge my presence so I sat down at the table opposite of her.

"I had a good nap. I feel a whole lot better now. That was the best sleep that I've had in a long time. Your bed smells so good."

"Thank you. I'm glad that you got your rest. I have the hot links on boiling. I was gonna wake you up as soon as they were ready."

"Good, I'm as hungry as a bear in the spring. "What do you think my chances are of getting on where you work?"

"They won't hire you at these laundries unless you're eighteen. They used to until a young girl got her hand hurt on the mangle. Now they're very strict."

"But I'll be eighteen next month. Do they check to see if you're telling the truth?"

"Yes, they sure do since that girl got hurt."

"Well it's okay because Gene said that he was going to take me around to the hotels and motels to look for work."

"Do you have any money?"

"Yes, I have enough to buy us some food for a couple of days," I said and laughed.

She didn't laugh. "How much is that?"

"I have six dollars."

"Mama sent you out here broke?"

"Mama and Granddaddy are just barely making it themselves. All they have is their old age pension, unless one of their children sends them a few dollars."

"That old lady has money. She will stretch a dollar until it hollers."

"Mama puts a lot of money into the church and helping people. She orders the Sunday School books and pays for them herself. She always says that she wants to 'live by the side of the road and be a friend to man'."

"Well even so, she shouldn't have sent you out here broke," she sneered.

"I'll have a job soon. Gene and I may go looking tomorrow. I was working back there, but I had to leave because my boss and her son were crazy folks. I had saved up some money before I left home, but I had to pay Johnnie to bring me."

"How much did you pay him?"

"Twenty-five dollars."

"Some people," she sneered. "He had to come back anyway. He could have let you ride for free."

"I didn't mind paying. Anything that is free is not worth having. I wouldn't have enjoyed my trip as much if I hadn't paid for it."

She got up and took two plates from the cabinet. She sat the plates on the table and put a hotlink on each. She put one in front of me and then gave me two slices of bread. We had a sandwich and washed it down with some Kool-aid.

"If you'll go to the store with me, I'll buy some food and cook us a good meal tomorrow," I said.

"I'm going to work tomorrow. Maybe Gene can take you. Did you have a boyfriend back home?"

"Yes, his name is Toby and he worked with me," I lied.

I was embarrassed to say that I didn't have a boyfriend at my age. But Mama had made it next to impossible for me to have a boyfriend. She interrogated every boy that ever showed any interest in me. Once it was a teacher's son. Almost every girl in high school liked him, but he asked me if he could come to see me and I said yes. I was sure that it would be all right with Mama because she let Alice take company when she turned sixteen. But the boys had to come to the house. Alice wasn't allowed to hang around the store front with them. But she did it anyway. When I told Mama about the teacher's son, she said sure, invite him over.

So one Sunday evening after church, I invited him over. Everything was going well until she came out on the porch and joined us.

"What are your intentions with my granddaughter?" she asked Bruce.

"What do you mean Ma'am?"

"Are you looking for a wife or are you just smelling around?"

He went back and told it. I was the laughing stock at school for a long time. So after that, I never brought anyone else home. I guess the reason that I said Toby was my boyfriend is because he had invited me to go to Chicago with him.

Alice snickered and asked, "Have you ever done the do?"

I laughed and answered, "Not really. I came close on Prom night but I didn't."

"What happened?"

"My date and I were parked on a dark road in his daddy's truck. The Law came and shined a flashlight on us and told us to go home."

"Were you all naked?"

"No, we were just kissing."

But that wasn't the truth either. That had happened to another girl and she'd told me about it. I was trying my best to impress Alice.

"You've got to stop saying 'The Law.' People are gonna laugh at you. Once you've crossed the Mason Dixon Line, the word is police, cop or sheriff."

"I'll try to remember that."

I'm not doing so good at impressing her.

I was very careful how I talked after that. After we finished our sandwiches and Kool-aid, I washed the dishes.

"I think that I'm gonna like having you around," she said.

"Thanks."

That made me feel real good. We sat and talked about home and watched television. She got at least three telephone calls, but each time she told the person on the other end, 'No not tonight, my little sister is here from out of town.' One of them must have told her to bring me because she looked at me and laughed. Then she said, 'I don't know if that's a good idea. I don't think she's ready yet.'

When we got ready to go to bed, I picked up my purse from the couch. It was open and my billfold was on top of everything else. I always kept it pushed way down so it wouldn't fall out. I opened my billfold and my six dollars were gone. The only money that I had in the world. Now she was going to think that I lied about having some money.

That man that was in here with her got it.

I dropped down on her couch and started crying. She came out of the bathroom and stood over me.

"What's wrong?"

"My six dollars is gone," I sobbed.

I looked up at her and sobbed, "I swear I had it."

"Maybe it fell out of your purse."

"It was in my billfold and the billfold is still here."

"Don't worry about it. I know where you can make forty dollars."

"Where?"

"Come on to bed, we'll talk about it tomorrow morning."

We went into the bedroom and went to bed. I wanted to talk about how I was going to make forty dollars, but she turned her back to me.

"I'm dog tired, good night."

"Good night," I said and turned my back to her.

I got over to the edge of the bed on my side to keep from touching against her. She had gotten in the bed stark naked and I didn't like that. To me, it was disrespectful.

Maybe when I get in touch with Ben, I can live with him and his family.

The next morning, the telephone woke us up. Alice answered it and went into the living room to talk. After she hung up, she made another call. She asked the person if he wanted some action that night. He must have said yes.

"Now it won't be me, it will be someone who looks like me."

The person said something and she answered, "You got it. What time? Now she gets the same deal that I get right? Forty bucks."

They talked a little while longer and she hung up. When she came back into the bedroom, I pretended to be asleep. She smoked a cigarette and got back in bed. After a while, I heard a light snore and I eased out of bed. I was starving, so I went into the kitchen to look for food. I thought when she said that she didn't have anything but the hot links, she really meant that they were the only thing she had that was easy to prepare. But there was nothing in her kitchen that even resembled food except a half loaf of bread, a little Kool-aid and a half jar of sandwich spread. She was even down to one can of beer. I made me a sandwich out of the sandwich spread and bread and poured me half a glass of the left over Kool-aid. I was afraid to take more.

When I finished eating, I tiptoed back into the bedroom and got my purse. I sat on the couch and took everything out, looking for my money. But it was gone, and I almost cried again. The only reason that I didn't was because I thought about the forty dollars that I was going to make.

That is really something. It would take me almost three weeks to make that much back home. And the way Alice sounds, I'm going to make it all at once. These people out here have money to burn.

I had heard that you could walk along the streets and find silver dollars. I wanted to watch television, but I didn't want to turn it on, for fear I might break it. So, I lay on the couch and tried to remember my dream. I could remember Mama coming into my room and telling me something, but what she said, just wouldn't come through. The more I tried to remember it, the further it slipped away. I dozed off on the couch because I didn't want to get back in the bed with Alice's naked body.

Later, I heard her taking a bath. I was glad that she was up because I was anxious to hear what she had to tell me. Finally, she came in the living room all made up and smelling good. She sat on the couch and I sat up straight.

"I don't have any food here because I wasn't expecting you. And since you've lost your money, I'm gonna loan you ten dollars so you can eat and have cab fare."

"Oh, I don't need that much. Just a few dollars will do. I can get Gene or Bertha to take me to the store. I don't need to take a taxicab."

"You'll need to take a cab tonight. Do you remember I told you that you could make forty dollars?"

"Yes, I remember."

"Well, I have it all set up. This guy is expecting you at eight o'clock tonight. Here is his address and telephone number."

She handed me a folded piece of paper and a ten dollar bill.

"And don't tell Gene or Bertha about this."

"Okay. But what kind of job is it? What do I have to do for this forty dollars?"

"Just keep him company. And if he wants you to do anything else, he'll tell you. Believe me, he's harmless. I'm going to work today, but I'm gonna leave my door key with you. I get off from work at nine o'clock so try to get back as soon as you can."

"Can I change my mind? I don't feel right about this."

"Why don't you feel right about it?"

"Nobody gives you that kind of money just to talk to them a little while. That guy is probably expecting me to have him. And I don't sell my body for money."

"Trust me when I tell you that having you is the furthest thing from this guy's mind."

After she said that, I just figured that this was some old decrepit, lonesome soul. And I would go there and sit and read to him.

"I'll do it. And I won't tell Gene or Bertha. But at least you'll know where I'm going just in case something happens."

"You'll be all right. And you don't have to give me but twenty dollars this time."

I looked at her, and she said, "My ten and ten more for the connection."

I put the money and the address in my purse and put my purse in the bedroom. I had this bad feeling that she was not on the level. She turned the television on, opened her last can of beer and lit a cigarette. I could see why she was so thin, she never ate. She was thinner than me and I only weighed one hundred and five pounds. She sat at the dinette table smoking and drinking. I went into the bedroom, dressed and made up the bed. I heard a knock at the door. She opened it and told Gene to come in. I hurried and finished the bed and rushed into the living room. I spoke to Gene and told him that I was just about to call him.

"I'm on my way to get something to eat and I stopped by to see if you wanted to go."

"Yes, but I thought we were going to look for a job this morning."

"I had planned to, but Bertha said to let you visit with Alice a day or two. But we can go tomorrow for sure."

"I'll be ready. Okay, let's go," I said grabbing my purse.

"Don't forget the key."

Alice took the door key off her key chain and handed it to me. "I'll be gone when you get back. But you know what to do."

I didn't answer her I just took the key and followed Gene out. We rode around the Westside in Bertha's car and then went to eat. After we ate, I got Gene to take me to Ben's house but there was nobody home. He brought me back to Alice's apartment and let me out.

"I'll see you tomorrow morning bright and early."

I went in and turned the television on the way I saw Alice do it. I watched television and finished my leftover food. That evening, I took a bath and put on my best clothes. At 7:30 p.m., I called a taxicab from the number that Alice left by the telephone. I locked the apartment door and waited for the taxicab outside. When the driver arrived, I got in the back seat and told him where I wanted to go.

"And can you tell me how much it's going to cost Sir?"

"I won't know until I get there. You must be new at this."

"Yes Sir, I just got here yesterday."

"And you're at it already?"

I didn't answer him because I didn't understand the question.

"Where are you from?"

"Canton, Mississippi."

"You know, I usually just collect my fares and keep my trap shut. But I'm going to go out on a limb here because I don't think you realize what you're getting yourself into. I know that address and you shouldn't be going there. How old are you, about fifteen?"

"No Sir, I'm almost eighteen. Why shouldn't I be going there?"

"If you don't already know right from wrong, me telling you won't do any good."

"Well I'm just going over there to read to this guy. My sister Alice said that he's lonesome and needs somebody to talk too."

"And you believe her?"

"Yes Sir, I do."

The driver didn't say anything else. When we got there, he pulled into the front of the motel and stopped. He looked over his shoulder and told me how much I owed. I paid him and got out.

He hollered, "Please be careful."

"Thank you Sir, I will."

I looked at the address again and went to find the door. I found the door but something told me, don't knock, go home. I was just about to walk away and take a taxicab back home, but two white men were walking toward me on the sidewalk. So I knocked on the door. A short pot-bellied man with jet black hair opened the door.

"Come in Meredith," he said smiling.

I was about to ask him how he knew my name.

Alice probably told him my name like she told me his.

I stepped inside and he said, "Come on and have a seat."

I walked over to the corner of the room and sat in a chair.

"What do you want to drink, beautiful?"

"Nothing, but I thank you just the same."
"Well I'm going to have one."
I didn't answer. He fixed his drink and sat on the foot of the bed facing me.
"Alice tells me that the two of you are sisters."
"Yes Sir, that's right."
"Alice and I have been friends for damn nigh four years."
"That's nice."
"That Alice sure has a lot of spunk. I like that in a woman."
He sprung up from the bed and asked, "Well shall we get started?"
"Get started doing what? I thought that I was here to talk to you and keep you company awhile."
He laughed and asked, "Is that what Alice told you?"
"Yes Sir, she did."
"Well we can talk awhile," he said and sat back down.
"So, how do you like Las Vegas so far? Alice tells me that you just got here from Mississippi."
"It's too soon to tell Sir."
"Let's drop the 'Sir' business," he said and extended his hand.
"My name is Pete."
I shook it and said, "My name is Meredith and I'm please to meet you."
"I'm from the South too. Louisiana. My folks own a sugarcane plantation down there. I got tired of the South and came to Las Vegas. I'm a dealer on the 'Strip.' I've been here a little over four years, but I haven't accumulated myself a girlfriend yet. I'm looking for someone like you. You know, you could pass for a Mexican or an Indian. You and Alice must be from one of the finer tribes in Africa."
"We were born and bred in Mississippi."
"I didn't mean that you-all were born in Africa, I meant your ancestors. But let's get off the subject. And forget what Alice told you. Do you want to make forty bucks?"

"No Sir, thank you. I better go."

By now, I knew what he was up to. And I knew that he wasn't going to give me forty dollars for a conversation. I was just hoping to make it out safe, because he was sitting between me and the door.

"All you have to do is hit me with a wet towel real hard and call me sweet names. And I'll give you the money. What do you say?"

I didn't answer. He got up and went into the bathroom and I heard water running. I tiptoed to the door and eased it open. He ran out of the bathroom naked and hollered, "Hey!"

But I was already out of the door. I walked around to the front of the motel and a taxicab was letting a couple out. I asked the driver if he would take me to the Westside.

"Hop in."

I got in on the back seat. I was glad that this guy was white. He didn't try to talk to me. I gave him the address and we rode in silence.

CHAPTER VIII

Mossy...

On my way to Dallas, I pondered the idea of whether to tell Ellen the truth. I wasn't afraid for myself anymore, because I wasn't ever going back home. And I knew Daddy well enough to know that he wouldn't come to Dallas.

Besides, I've shown him that I'm no longer a push over. I don't think he wants to tangle with me anymore. He knows now that I'm not going to stand still and let him kill me. But I hate to involve Ellen and make her get into it with him. And, I sure don't want Mama drawn into it. She might lose the little mind she has. I wish I could talk to a priest. If I don't tell somebody, I'm going to lose my mind. It's a wonder that I've lasted this long. Daddy had no right to do this to me, this is a mess.

I was still debating when the bus pulled into the terminal in Dallas. When the driver announced 'Dallas' over the loud speaker, my heart fluttered. I stayed in my seat until everybody who was getting off, had gotten off. Then I picked up my overstuffed pillowcase and carried it in the front of me. There was a soldier standing outside on the ground and he helped me get it off of the bus. After thanking him, I went into the station and found a telephone. I dialed Ellen's number, not expecting her to be home. I knew that she should be at work. But, I checked just the same. There was no answer, so I went to the food counter and ordered a sandwich and a Coca-Cola. It cost a lot more than I had expected.

At this rate my money is not going to last long.

After I finished eating, I bought a comic book and sat and read it. After I finished reading, I sat and watched the goings-ons in the station. The bus station bums were in and out looking for an easy prey. I saw one sleeping traveler get his bus ticket stolen right out of his hands. After a while, a little Mexican boy walked up to me carrying a young baby.

"Senora, can you give me some money to buy milk for the baby?"

"My Mama left the baby and me and she just never came back."

I opened my purse and gave him fifty-cents. Then I got up and moved to another seat near people. The bums seemed to be looking for people who were alone.

After several tries, I finally reached Ellen. When I told her that I was in Dallas, she thought I was kidding.

"I'm really here," I assured her, "and I've been here for hours."

"You're going to have to take a taxicab here. My car is in the shop."

"Okay, there are some outside."

I got my pillowcase and went outside and caught a taxicab. I got into the back seat and gave him Ellen's address. When I got there, I paid the driver, grabbed my pillowcase and got out. I didn't have to knock on Ellen's apartment door because she had been watching out for me. She let me in and gave me a big hug. I held onto her tight and fought back the tears.

"Have a seat and tell me why you're here carrying a pillowcase."

I told her point blank, “I ran away and I’m not going back. No, I take that back. Daddy ran me away. I’m tired of lying. The chips can fall where they may.”

She sat down beside me and said, “Slow down and tell me what happened and I want you to start from the beginning.”

“If I do that, it will take all night,” I said trying to hold back my tears, “because I’d have to go back eight years.”

“Then what happened today,” she said impatiently.

“He tried to have sex with me, so I pulled his shotgun on him and he told me to get out.”

“Daddy tried to have you?”

“Yes,” I cried, “and he has been doing it off and on ever since I was ten.”

“I can’t believe what I’m hearing.”

“Why didn’t you tell me, even if you didn’t want to tell Mama.”

“Because I couldn’t,” I cried. “He said that he would kill me and anybody that I told.”

She put her arm around me and said, “Stop crying, it’s going to be all right now that you’re here with me.”

“Ellen, you can’t say anything about this, he will kill us. He told me that he would die before he goes back to the pen.”

“I won’t say anything to anybody about this. You can trust me. Have I ever lied to you about anything important?”

“No.”

“But it’s not because I’m afraid of what he will do to us. I’m keeping quiet for Mama’s sake. This could push her over the edge. And Daddy don’t have long before he has to account for his deeds.”

“What do you mean?”

“Daddy is a whole lot sicker than he is letting on.”

“Me, myself, I believe that he has cancer and that’s why he don’t want to go to the doctor. He’s afraid of what he’s going to hear. When I look in his eyes, I see pain. And poor

Mama doesn't deserve this," she said shaking her head. "She's in the shape that she's in today because of his foolishness."

"What do you mean?" I asked.

"She's scatterbrain because of him. She tried to stop the Marshal from arresting him for cattle rustling because she knew he wasn't guilty. The Marshal hit her upside her head with the butt of his rifle and knocked her out of the way. I was little, but I can remember blood being everywhere. Mama never did recover from that. Later on, she had a nervous break-down. She was so proud of you when you were born. Everybody thought she would snap out of it. And it seemed like she had for a while, but she soon started regressing."

"Nobody has ever explained it to me like this before."

"I told you that Mama had a nervous break-down when you were complaining about her not paying attention to you."

"I know you did and so did Aunt Florence. You all also told me that she wasn't herself. But I didn't know what any of it meant, not really. She was forty-five when she had me so I thought she just didn't want me."

"The sad thing about all of it is the whole thing was senseless. Daddy wasn't trying to steal no cow. He and two other old fools got drunk on moonshine and made a bet about which one would have sex with the cow. They all got caught, but the white man got the other two to testify against Daddy because he saw a chance to take our land. Daddy was the only one who did any time. Robert Jr. and Joseph would have ended up killing those other two men if they had stayed around Marlin, so Mama's brother in Compton sent for them to keep them out of trouble. Then Rachel and Sarah moved to Compton. We didn't farm anymore after Daddy got sent up. His foolishness changed everything for us. Where was Mama when all of this happened?"

"The same place she always is, in town peddling."

"Mossy, I'm so sorry this happened to you. Aunt Florence always says, 'All family ain't good family. Sometimes you have to play the hand you get.' I never understood what she meant until now."

"But why did I have to draw this hand?"

"I wish I knew."

I felt better after I cried and let everything out. We sat and talked for a long time. I told her about the first time Daddy raped me and every other time that I could think about. I even told her about what he had done to Ruben James.

Ellen finally asked me, "What are your plans now?"

"To stay here in Dallas and find a job."

"At least let me tell Mama where you are so she won't worry."

"Okay, you can tell her."

"I don't think as hard of her as I did before we talked."

"What about college? Mama made me promise that if anything happened to her, I would make sure you still got to college."

"I can't think about college now. It's a relief to be away from any academic studies. You don't know what school was like for me. It was very tedious. And now that I've made it through, I want a break, a long break."

Ellen looked sad. I hated to see her looking that way, so I patted her on her knee.

"Don't worry, I'm going to college. Just not right now. I want to make some money so I can buy some nice clothes. Just about everything I have Mama or Aunt Florence made for me. And anyway, my teacher said that it's okay to rest, but just don't quit. He said that if you don't go to college before you're thirty that you're not likely to go. But I'm going way before I'm thirty. I might start in the fall of 1961. So, are you going to help me find a job?"

"Yes, I'm trying to think where to look."

"What about at the department store where you work?"

“No, that will never do. My boss wouldn’t allow it. He don’t hire kin folks because he thinks they may conspire to steal. But I’ll check around and see what I can come up with for you.”

***

It was two weeks before Ellen came home and told me that she’d found something that she thought I’d be good at. During that two week period, I cooked, cleaned her one bedroom apartment and took long walks. Sometimes I stopped and talked to anybody who would talk to me. I knew people around there who Ellen didn’t even know.

The job she found for me was in the kitchen of an exclusive restaurant in downtown Dallas. The large dining area was called the Neptune Room. The food was gourmet and very expensive. It was reported that the walls and ceiling were painted by some famous artist. The whole area except the kitchen gave you the feeling of dining under the sea. It was truly magnificent. It was a place where well-to-do white folks came to enjoy the food and socialize with their peers. The customers consisted of lawyers, doctors and business men and women from the downtown area. But a few of the customers were not so well-to-do lonely ladies. They came and paid those exorbitant prices in hopes of meeting a rich business man.

There were two regulars. They came two or three times a week and always ordered the breakfast. The waitresses would laugh at them. They said for what they were paying for a plate of bacon, eggs, toast, and coffee, they could buy groceries and get a pound of bacon, a whole loaf of bread, a dozen eggs and a pound of coffee. Even though they came around lunch time, the manager would let them order breakfast just the same. He got a kick out of them. They were always so well dressed. He said that they gave zest to the place.

My job was to make club sandwiches and to help out wherever I was needed. It seemed that the kitchen was full of black people. Actually, there were only seven in there, and eight if you counted the Maitre D' who was always in and out. His name was Myron and he gave suave a new meaning. He called all the women "Honey", "Baby" or "Sweetness." When he wasn't busy, he was in the kitchen with us gossiping and dipping his hand in the food. His uniform fitted him to the T and he thought that he was hot shit. He was the only black who went out in the front around the customers.

When the boss first introduced me around, he told Miss Pearl that he was leaving me in her hands. She was the oldest of the kitchen helpers, and the most trusted one. She had the key to the stockroom, but she couldn't read a lick. She always had to take somebody with her to help her fill the chef's orders. After I started, she would always take me. Melvin was the chef and Ethan was his back-up and flunky. But Miss Pearl also knew her way around in the kitchen. She had the biggest hips and they would shake like jelly. I always walked behind on our way to and from the stockroom, just because I liked to watch her hips jolt up and down.

She told me about everybody's business while we were in the stockroom. But she admitted that she didn't know much about Myron because he kept his business to himself and talked about everybody else's. I made sure that she wasn't going to be able to tell my business. Everything I told her except names was made-up or exaggerated. When she asked about my parents, I told her that they owned a ranch and my mother taught school. And on the subject of my siblings, I told her that they were all professionals. But she wouldn't leave it alone; she asked what fields were they in. I had to think fast. Sarah was easy because she is a nurse, but I had to find jobs for the other four and I even forgot what I said except that I told her Robert Jr. was a doctor in Los

Angeles. I was trying to impress her, but I made her jealous instead.

"If your folks got so much, why are you working here?"

I came up with an answer without even having to think. "Because I'm going to college next year to study nutrition and I want to work around food for a while before I start."

She never asked me anything else about my family. Soon after I started to work, Melvin had to leave to have surgery on his hand, so they hired a substitute named Wayne. He was a small guy and not quite as tall as me. He was a good cook but the rumor was that he was a closet drunkard. He set his sight on me right away. He was at my station talking to me every chance he got. And if the boss came through, he would keep talking. Miss Pearl told me that he was going to get me and himself fired. After that, I was very uncomfortable talking to him. I avoided him as much as possible, but he just couldn't catch a hint. Most of the time when he tried to talk to me, I didn't answer him. And if I got half a chance, I'd walk away. When he saw that he wasn't getting anywhere with me, he became hostile and started saying disrespectful things to me.

Before Miss Pearl had said anything about getting fired, he had slipped me three or four deep-fried shrimps quite a few times. I would hide and eat them. But after she said that, I told him that I didn't want anymore.

"What's the matter, have you all of a sudden lost your taste for shrimps?" he sneered.

"As a matter of fact, I have!" I snapped back.

He walked back over to where Ethan was and whispered something to him and they both laughed.

I asked Miss Pearl out loud, "When do you think Melvin will be back?"

"He could be out for a month or two."

"Well I don't know if I can last that long."

Before long, Ethan was in on the act. He told me that Wayne said that my titties were driving him wild and he wanted to grab one of them in his mouth and run under a pillow with it.

"Well, don't let Wayne use your mouth for a garbage can," I sneered.

The next morning while Miss Pearl and I were in the stockroom, I told her, "I can't take too much more of Wayne. I might just quit before he makes me hurt him."

"Don't quit. I need you. You're a nice girl and you're the first young person who didn't poke fun at me when you found out that I couldn't read. Let me tell Mr. Russell on him."

"No, that may make matters worse. I'll just ask him real nice to leave me alone."

"Okay, but be careful because Wayne drinks heavy. But the only time he shows it is when he gets upset. I've worked with him before at a restaurant. He does his best cooking after he has had a little nip."

"Thanks for the warning."

Wayne passed by me that evening looking at my breasts and licking his tongue out.

I mumbled, "You drunken bastard, I hate you." I just couldn't help myself.

The next morning, he was late for work. Miss Pearl was getting set to help Ethan so she told me that we had to hurry up in the stockroom. But just as we got back to the kitchen, Wayne came stumbling through the kitchen door. And this time, even I could tell that he was drunk. He apologized for being late and went in the back and put on his uniform. When he got back, he stood in the middle of the floor.

"You all listen up," he said in a loud slurred voice. "Everybody's name that I call gets their choice of a steak or shrimps for breakfast."

He called everybody's name but mine.

"Now everybody who wants a steak, raise your hand and tell me how you like it," he slurred.

Myron was the only one who raised his hand. He told Wayne that he wanted his steak medium well.

"Now everybody who wants big ole delicious deep-fried shrimps, raise your hands," he slurred.

But nobody raised their hands that time. Myron had gone back out front. Wayne went back to his station and started working. But soon, he got sick and had to run out of the kitchen. Ethan went to see about him. He came back and said that Wayne was throwing up. When Wayne got back, he appeared to be in a better shape. He took charge of the cooking and Ethan assisted him. Everything ran smooth until breakfast was over.

When Myron finished his work out front, he came into the kitchen. He walked up to Wayne.

"I finally got caught up and now I'll have that steak. And I'll take a few fries with it if you don't mind."

I really believe that Wayne had forgot that he had promised Myron a steak because his purpose was to feed everybody but me to make me feel bad. But since everybody had declined except Myron, it was of no benefit to him. He looked at Myron through blood shot eyes.

"Man what in the hell are you talking about?"

"I'm talking about that steak that you promised me this morning. Right after you came in this morning, you asked who wanted steak and who wanted shrimps, and I said steak."

Myron looked around at the others for support but nobody said anything because they knew that Wayne was not supposed to be feeding the help shrimps and steaks.

"Man get the fuck out of my face," Wayne scoffed.

"Come on Man. I didn't ask you for no steak, you asked me."

"I said get the fuck out of my face! Why in the fuck would I give you a steak? Is this your fucking birthday or something?"

"Come on man," Myron begged. "I'm hungry and a promise is a promise."

"Just stand right there," Wayne scoffed, "I've got your steak and your promise too."

He rushed over to a table and grabbed a meat cleaver. Ethan hollered "Hold it there man, you don't want to do that!"

"Get out of my way!" he yelled to Ethan. "I told that mother fucker to leave me alone."

When Myron saw the meat cleaver, he ran pass me toward the dining room door. Wayne was holding the cleaver like he was going to throw it, so I ran too, right behind Myron. Miss Pearl and the others ran out behind me. We ran out in the front to the waitresses' station. Myron told them that Wayne was after him with a knife. One of the waitresses ran to tell the boss. There were a few customers who had lingered over from breakfast. They were talking and drinking coffee. When they saw us run out of the kitchen, they started asking if there was a fire. The waitresses quickly assured them that there was no fire and that they weren't in danger.

When the boss came out, he came through the kitchen and told everybody to go back to work except Myron, Miss Pearl and me. He told us to come with him and he took us back through the kitchen. I didn't see Wayne, but Ethan was busy working. The boss took us to his office and asked us what was going on. Miss Pearl spoke up and tried to put everything on me. She told the boss that there was something going on between Wayne and me. And he had been drinking because he was upset with me.

"I think she let him down pretty hard and Myron just tried to talk to Wayne at the wrong time and got caught up in it."

I was looking at her while she was talking. But she wouldn't look at me, she kept looking away. I got so angry that I blurted out, "That's not the truth! She's taking up for Wayne! That's not what happened, Sir."

The boss said in a pleasant, but firm voice, "Then why don't you tell me what happened young lady. And I want the truth."

He had been sitting up straight at his desk. But now he was leaning back in his chair with his eyes fixed on me. Everybody's eyes were on me, so I looked down as I talked.

"Wayne has been trying to like me ever since he came. And at first I didn't say nothing because I didn't want to hurt his feelings. But Miss Pearl told me that he was going to get me fired, so I asked him nice to leave me alone. But he got mad and started meddling me."

"What do you mean about meddling you?"

"Saying things and touching me."

"Well why didn't you come in here and tell me?"

But before I could answer him, Miss Pearl spoke and put her foot right in her mouth. "I told her to tell you and even offered to come in here with her."

"So you did know about Wayne bothering this girl?"

"I saw them talking, but I didn't know nothing about no touching."

"We'll talk about this later," he said to her.

Then he turned his attention back to me. "What were you going to tell me about why you didn't come to me?"

"Because I didn't know that it would come to this Sir."

"I thought Melvin would be back and Wayne would be gone."

He looked at Myron and asked, "What was your involvement in this? They told me that you ran out first and it was you that he was chasing with the knife."

"Yes Sir, it was. But it wasn't my fault. He promised to fix me breakfast. And when I caught up out front, I went back there and told him that I was ready for my breakfast. But he flew off the handle and grabbed the meat cleaver."

"You can go on back to work and you too Pearl."

Both of them got up and walked out. I got real worried because I knew that I was going to get all of the blame. After the door was closed behind them, the boss sat up straight again. He looked away from me, let out a sigh and looked back at me.

“Young lady, I hate to put you out on the street. But let’s face it, you don’t fit in back there and I’ve got a business to run here. I just can’t tolerate this kind of interruption.” He sighed again and said real fast, “I’m letting you go and good luck in finding a job. You can use me as a reference if you like. I’m sorry, but I just can’t take chances. If this had happened during the lunch hour when the dining room was full, it would have been a mess. You can go around to personnel and pick up your pay. And again, good luck to you.”

I got up and said, “Thank you Sir,” and left.

I went back to where we kept our belongings, got my purse and took my apron off. Then I went to get my pay. I walked to the bus stop thinking this is a scary world. It seems like no matter what it is, I’m always standing alone. I would like to have known what happened to Wayne, but I had no way of finding out.

CHAPTER IX

Alice...

Seeing Meredith again after four years made me realize what this fast life had done to my looks. She looked so young and pretty. Before I had met Jeff, I used to look like that too. Like her, I looked a lot younger than my years. I gave Meredith a warm greeting when she got here and tried not to show my resentment, but it wasn't easy. Bertha and Gene were watching me closely and I believe they saw right through me, especially Gene because he was always on me about my looks. He would always ask, "Why don't you get some sleep? Then you wouldn't have to wear all of that gunk on your face."

But he left me alone after I got mad and told him off. "You need to work on losing some weight and stop worrying about how I look," I sneered. "And what do you know anyway? Your fat ass is eighteen years old and you still haven't decided whether you wanna be male or female."

He didn't respond to that, he just said, "I'll see you when you're in a better mood," and left.

After he left, I felt lousy because I knew that he couldn't help the way that he was. I guess he figured that it would take awhile for me to be in a better mood. He stopped coming around for about four months, and I missed him like hell. He was the only member of my family who ever visited and the only one who accepted me for who I was.

That's why I was so glad to see Meredith. Now, I'd have two people who cared about me. Although I was happy that she was here, I couldn't help but resent her fresh, wholesome look. She made me feel like I was over the hill and I was just twenty-two. Before now, I had never dwelled on my looks. Some mornings when I looked in the mirror, I would scare myself. Sometimes I had bags under my eyes large enough to tote something in. But I just got my cold teaspoon out of the refrigerator and pressed them down. Then I'd throw on some extra make-up and keep on going. But now that she was here, I knew that people would start comparing us.

I'm gonna have to start getting some rest and taking better care of myself. Hopefully I can get her broken in and let her see some of my clients. That way, I can get some rest and still get half of the money. With her wholesome look, I know the Johns will go crazy over her.

She was real tired from the trip, so I let her take a nap in my bed. When Naomi came by to pick me up for work, I went out to her car to tell her that my sister was here and I wasn't going in. I could see the jealous look on her face. She thought that I had finally gotten a little happiness and she wanted to rain on my parade. "Guess who I saw last night," she said.

"Who?"

"Jeff and Jean. They were walking around in Vegas Village holding hands. I tried to tell you that he was lying to you and he was back with the bitch."

She wanted to hurt my feelings and keep me from getting mad at her, all at the same time. She had never called Jean a bitch before. When I talked to her about Jean, she would say, 'Well what do you expect Alice? She had him first. You stole him from her.' I was already upset about Meredith and she added insult to injury. But I stayed cool and tried not to show that I was hurt.

"Thanks for telling me. But Gene beat you to the draw. He had already told me. But to be perfectly honest with you, I don't give a rat's ass what Jeff does anymore. My sister is here now and she's gonna stay here with me. I don't even want to be associated with the likes of Jeff and Jean. He can have her crippled ass. They deserve each other. I'm above both of them."

"Well if you say so. You enjoy your sister's company and I'll see you tomorrow." Then she sped away.

When I got back inside, I sat down and smoked a cigarette to calm my nerves. While I was smoking, I got a brainstorm. I got up and looked in on Meredith and she was sound asleep. So, I pulled the bedroom door closed and started my scheme. She had left her purse on my couch.

She always was too trusting and lucky for me she still is. She hasn't been out of the woods long enough to know that you keep your money close to you.

When I opened her purse and took out her billfold, there was only six dollars in it.

No wonder she left her purse lying around, there ain't nothing in it but chicken feed. She's got her big money tied to her bra strap, and there ain't no way for me to get it without waking her up.

So I took the six dollars and decided I would have to find a way to get the big money later. I needed to make her broke and desperate for my scheme to work. A broke person was a desperate person. And a desperate person was easier to persuade.

But I have to work on her fast. I have to get her initiated before Ben finds out that she is here. He knows what I'm doing because Jean and Blanche told him. But they made it sound worse than it is. They told him that I turn tricks and give every penny to Jeff. So, I know that when Ben finds out that Meredith is here with me, he is gonna try to talk her against me and we're gonna be in a tug-of-war over Meredith. But if I can set her up with a trick before she sees Ben, she will keep her mouth shut and I can pull her over to my side. I hope I can get back the control over her that I had back home.

She was so easy to control when we were growing up. All I had to do was to give her the evil eye, raise my voice, or act impatient. It didn't take long before she was hollering 'Okay, okay, okay.' She never did like a conflict. But I did, if I thought I could win.

I was concentrating on my scheme so hard that I'd forgotten all about what Naomi had told me about Jeff. Then out of the clear blue, he knocked on my door. He couldn't have come at a better time because this was my opportunity to find out how he really felt about me. I let him in and whispered to him to talk low.

"Why?" he asked out loud.

"I have company dummy," I whispered and pointed to my bedroom.

"I'm glad to see that you've found yourself somebody," he sneered. "Is it anybody I know?"

"No, you don't know this person," I sneered back.

"Well, I saw your light on, so I decided to stop by and get that package. I'll take it if you have it handy, so I can get out of you-all's way."

Those words cut like a knife but I went on and said, "It's not what you think. It's my sister Meredith in there sleeping. She came out here to live with me."

I walked over to the table, sat down and lit a cigarette. He got all happy and sat down in the chair across from me.

"That's nice," he said smiling. "Why didn't you say that at first? I'd like to meet her."

"She's asleep. She's tired from that long ride out here."

"Well some other time. I'll take that package and go. I'm getting something else lined up for you. I'll call you with the information."

I didn't answer him. I just blew out a puff of smoke and looked straight pass him. "How much is it?" he asked.

"I can't spare it Jeff. I need it to help my sister."

That started the verbal fight. When I told him that I was quitting the business, he finally gave up, called us both a choice name and left.

As soon as he left, I put some hotlinks on to boil and sat down to figure out my next move. I felt good about the way I had handled the situation. I had hit him where it hurt, right in his pocket. With him out of the way, I could start my own business with Meredith. I had to find out a little more about her as soon as she got up. Four years is a long time and I didn't know how much she had changed. I had to find out if she had been giving up the cooch. If she hadn't, I'd start her off with Pete.

By the time the hotlinks were ready, she had gotten up. I sat there cool and reserved. I remembered her telling me that it bothered her when I wouldn't talk. I was setting the right mood to make her tell me everything I wanted to know. I fed her and started her to talking. In a few minutes, I found out everything I needed to know. I was happy to find out that I did have all of her money. Everything was working just the way I planned it. I was waiting for her to miss her money before I told her about the plan. When she found out that it was gone and started crying, I felt a little sorry for her. But I knew that I wasn't gonna let her go hungry, and you can't make an omelet without breaking eggs. My way, she would have forty dollars instead of six, minus my cut which would be ten. I decided that was all I would take from her first time out. Although I was brilliant, I was still surprised that she agreed so easily. I mean who did she think she was, for somebody to pay forty dollars to get into her stupid head. But I went to bed feeling proud of myself. I could tell that she wanted to talk some more, but I had everything that I wanted from her. I didn't want to talk. I wanted to lie in bed and think.

If this works, I'm home free. After the first time, I'll get half of everything she makes. And I can keep the money that I was giving to Jeff. Then I can save up some money and get myself into some kind of school. This was supposed to be a short term gig. I don't wanna be no old wrinkled up hooker. When I see the ones around here, I feel sorry for them. I'm determined not to be one of them. I owe it to myself and to Nicolas.

I promised him that I wasn't gonna get back into this line of work and that I wasn't going back to Jeff. But he had just barely touched down in New York and I was back into it.

But this time, Meredith and I will make some fast money and get out for sure. The only thing that bothers me about the whole thing is how Meredith is gonna act when she does see Ben. I know that I can't keep her from seeing him. And I'm worried that she will choose him over me, just like she chose our grandparents over me when we were small.

When my daddy used to leave us alone in that house in Canton, I took care of her. I felt needed and it was a good feeling. I didn't ever hit her except on her hand to make her leave things alone that could hurt her. I could have hit her any time I wanted to and there wouldn't have been anything done about it. Our daddy didn't care about us. He used us until he got tired of us and then he left us.

I used to call Meredith my baby. But when we went to live with my grandparents, she stopped coming to me. When something was wrong with her, she ran to them and that made me mad. I resented her and my grandparents because of it. After a while, I started knocking the hell out of Meredith and making trouble for her. I was trying my best to turn my grandparents against her so that she would turn back to me. Both of us peed the bed, but I figured out a way to put it all on Meredith.

At first, Mama didn't whip us about peeing in the bed. She just started giving us corn silk tea three times a day. Usually, it was before we went to school, right after school and later in the evening. She would sweeten the tea with honey, but I didn't like the taste of the tea or the honey. So if Mama didn't watch me, I didn't drink it. If I couldn't pour it out, I made Meredith drink it. She would gulp it down like she didn't have any taste buds. Soon, her weak bladder got better. She only peed the bed occasionally. But I peed every night. We were peeing out mattresses so fast that Mama and Aunt Amanda started making our mattresses. Sometimes it would be filled with whipped cotton and some corn shucks.

But when our room started stinking, Mama started whipping us. Of course each of us tried to put the peeing on the other one. So Mama started whipping whoever's gown was wet. I would wait until she blew the lamp out and then wrap my gown around my neck. The next morning the bed would be wet and Meredith's gown would be wet. But my gown would be dry. Sometimes Meredith got a whipping and sometimes, it was just a promise of a whipping. The promise was worse because that meant that they were piling up and Mama never forgot how many she owed you. This went on until our cousins and the other children started calling us pee babies. I got shamed and started drinking the tea without the honey. I didn't find out until years later that the honey served a purpose too.

No matter how much trouble I concocted for Meredith, our grandparents still favored her. So I just kept on beating her every chance I got until I got some kind of control over her. After I got some control over her, I felt better. I would make her steal things that we weren't supposed to bother. Then I would give her a small amount of it and she got blamed for it. Only once did she blatantly resist me. But even I had to laugh.

We were in this white man's pasture stealing pecans when his overweight bull dog came after us. We were almost to the fence when I tripped and fell. The dog was gaining on me so I hollered to Meredith to stop and get me a stick. 'Get one yourself,' she yelled back and scrambled under the fence. I guess her survival instinct was a little stronger than my control over her.

The night I sent her to see Pete, I felt good until it was almost time for me to get off from work. And then I started to worry. I knew that if I failed, I may not get another chance. On my way home, I hoped for the best, but I expected the worst.

CHAPTER X

Meredith...

When I got back to the apartment, I let myself in and sat down on the couch.

Son-of-a-gun, I'm not going to make it out here. Because no matter what, I'm not going to let Alice use me. I'm not that little girl that she used to hit and tell what to do. I would rather run back home with my tail tucked between my legs than to let her have me out in the streets hustling.

There was a knock on the door, so I got up and looked through the curtain. It was Alice. I took a deep breath and braced myself to stand up to her. I opened the door and the first thing out of her mouth was, "Well?"

"Well what?" I asked, trying to appear calm. I didn't want to get put out in the middle of the night.

"Did you get the money?"

"No, it wasn't as cut and dry as you claimed, so I left." She just walked pass me, sat down at the table and lit a cigarette. I closed the door and sat back down on the couch.

"Don't you worry. I'm going to get a job and pay you everything that I owe you."

She didn't answer me, but I could tell that she was angry. She got up, turned the television on and sat back down. I wanted to make her say something, so I said, "I went by to see Ben today, but they weren't home. He sure does have a big beautiful home. And I bet you miss not living there."

"As a matter of fact, I don't miss the house or him neither," she sneered. "And I sure as hell don't miss those little half-raised bitches of his."

I pressed it a little farther to let her know that I didn't believe her. "Well, I sure would like to live there."

Then I decided not to press my luck too far. I had stood my ground and won, at least for the moment. But with Alice, who knew what tomorrow would bring. I got up and said, "I think I'll turn in, good night."

She didn't answer me, but I saw her from the corner of my eyes, rolling her eyes at me. She didn't come to bed, she slept on the couch. But I still didn't get much sleep. I tossed and turned most of the night, worrying about being away from home and broke. I didn't know what to expect from Ben when I saw him because there were quite a few years between us and we were never close.

I was up before the alarm went off the next morning. I bathed, got dressed and called Gene. When he answered, I said, "I just wanted to make sure that you were up and we're still going job hunting."

"We sure are," he said in a feminine voice.

"Who is this?"

"It's me," he said and laughed. "I was just trying out my new voice."

"What are you talking about?"

"You will see when we get there. Bertha is off today and she's taking us."

"Oh good, I'll be ready when you-all get here," I said and hung up.

Alice was asleep on the couch so I pulled a chair up to the window and sat there looking out at the passing cars.

When Bertha's car pulled up, I put the chair back, dashed out of the door and locked it. When I got out to the car, I couldn't believe my eyes. Gene was sitting in the back seat dressed like a woman. And he had on a wig longer than the one that Bertha was wearing. I was standing there with my mouth open and they were laughing their heads off.

"Well, get in," Bertha said. I got in on the front seat and started laughing too.

"Well, how do I look?"

"You look good."

"But I still can't believe it. Why are you dressed like that?"

"I'm going to apply for a maid's job along with you."

"Good! I hope that it works. Then we can keep each other company."

I was surprised because I always thought that he was embarrassed about being gay. But it was good to know that he was okay with it, because I sure didn't mind. In school, we learned that each person is born with male and female hormones. So I figured that Gene's had just gotten screwed up somehow.

Bertha took us around to about three or four big hotels, but none of them were hiring, so she tried the motels. The second one we went to had openings and Gene and I applied. There was an older black lady taking applications. She gave us each one and told us to have a seat and fill them out. Gene was wearing a pair of Bertha's pumps and he tripped on his way to his seat. The old lady looked up and then kept on with her work. I finished my application and waited for Gene. We turned them in together. He had printed his name 'G. Adams'. The lady looked my application over first, and then looked at Gene's.

"What does the 'G' stand for?"

"Gene," he answered in a feminine voice.

She asked if we could start the next morning at eight and we answered yes, so she gave us a W-2 form to fill out. We completed the forms and turned them in. She told us that she would see us the next morning. Everything had gone well until we walked away from the desk. Gene stumbled again and this time, one of his pants legs fell down from under the skirt and the lady saw it. We hurried outside hoping that she hadn't noticed it, but she had. We thought that we had gotten over on her. We laughed our heads off all the way to the car.

Bertha was glad when we told her that we got the job. She told Gene that he was going to have to buy his own wardrobe. Everything he had worn to the interview was hers right down to the brassiere. He looked like an overweight prostitute in Bertha's clothes. Bertha treated us to lunch and took me home. She told me to be ready at a quarter after seven the next morning because she was going to drop us off on her way to work. Alice's ride had just pulled up when I got home. I was glad that she was leaving her own place. I told her that I had a job, but she seemed disinterested. I thought that it was probably because she wanted to turn me into a prostitute. I was trying hard not to hate her but she wasn't helping things.

I took my stationery out of my luggage and wrote Mama a letter. I told her that I was doing fine and I had already found a job. I let her know that I would be sending some money home soon. 'Alice is letting me stay with her,' I wrote. 'She has a real nice apartment and all of the modern gadgets, like a television, telephone, electric stove, and hot and cold running water. Her apartment looks like white folks live in it. I think that I'm going to like Las Vegas just fine. Kiss Granddaddy for me and tell him to please go to see Gloria as often as he can. I'll send some extra money for gas. Tell Aunt Amanda hello and that Johnnie, Bertha and Gene made it back safe. I haven't seen Ben yet, but I will go to see him soon. He and his family are well. And I heard that they both have a good job. I love you and Granddaddy and I miss you already. I will close my letter, but not my love. Your Granddaughter, Meredith. P.S. They have electric lights like you wouldn't believe downtown and on the "Strip".' I put the letter in my purse, so I could mail it the next day.

I slept and watched television the rest of the day and that evening I called Ben. He was beside himself when I said, "Hello Ben, it's me Meredith and I'm here in Las Vegas at Alice's apartment."

"Get ready, and I will be by to pick you up," he said excitedly. "Where is Alice?"

"She's at work."

"Good! I'll be there soon."

After we hung up, I combed my hair and put on the dress that I wore the night before. I sat at the window watching for him and when he got there, he didn't have to knock. I opened the door right away. We spoke, hugged and kissed and he lifted me off the floor. He sat down and I stood over him talking to him. I even touched his shoulder a couple of times. I just couldn't keep my hands off him. I felt so proud of him. He was so tall and good looking. And just to think that he was my blood brother.

Gloria had said that he looked like our daddy. And for the first time, I wished that I could remember what our daddy looked like. Ben looked around Alice's apartment and said, "This is nice, she has good taste. But she just doesn't have any common sense."

I laughed and said, "You can say that again. Go ahead and look around."

He got up and looked in her bedroom and said, "She took ways after that crazy S.O.B. that sired us. This is the first time that I've been here. I've completely washed my hands of her. And I hope that you won't stay here and let her ruin your reputation."

"I won't. I promise. I found a job today. And as soon as I get on my feet, I'm moving. I don't even want to be here now, but I just can't do any better."

I was hinting for him to say that I could come and live with him and his family, but he just said, “Let’s go, Laura is holding dinner for us.”

I locked the door and we left. On the way to his house, we talked about Gloria, our grandparents, and our people back home.

When I walked into his house, I was flabbergasted. It was beautiful. Laura and the girls greeted me at the door and I could smell fried chicken.

“I thought that Alice’s place was nice, but this takes the cake. I thought that only white folks lived like this. And you even have a piano.”

“Can you play?” Laura asked.

“A little. I played the one at our church. They don’t much care what you sound like, as long as you make some noise and it’s loud.”

I sat on the couch and Lucy sat on one side of me and Joyce sat on the other. They were both trying to talk to me at the same time. Joyce put her hands over my ears so I couldn’t hear what Lucy was saying. Pretty soon they got to fighting and Laura had to holler at them. She sent them to wash up for dinner. I got up and went into the kitchen where she and Ben were. Ben was helping Laura in the kitchen.

I asked if I could help, but Laura said, “No, you’ve had enough of our children already.”

But I had to admit, they were cute little girls. Laura is high yellow and Ben is brown. Between the two, they made beautiful offspring, but they were spoiled rotten.

We had a good meal and I helped Laura clean the kitchen. Laura’s cousin Corrine and her husband Kenneth came before we finished the kitchen. Ben entertained Kenneth and Corrine joined us in the kitchen.

This is just the way I’m going to live some day. I’m going to have a good man, a nice house, and invite family over. Hopefully, I’ll have some babies running around too.

Corrine was attending school to be a Licensed Practical Nurse. She also worked part-time as a nurse's aide. I listened carefully to her and Laura's conversation. I could tell that Laura was jealous of Corrine trying to better herself because she was just a housekeeper on the Strip. Even though a housekeeper was a step up from being a maid, it was not as good as being a nurse. Corrine was half bragging but that was no reason for Laura to cut her down the way she did. She told her that a LPN was a R.N.'s maid.

"Ben tried to get me to be a nurse. But I told him no way. And I sure wasn't going to be a nurse's aide. I can't stand the smells around the hospital. And I heard that the doctors treat you like dirt."

"Well the doctors I have met so far have been nice. And this is what I want to do."

They soon got on another subject, but I was still thinking about how much I would like to be a nurse. Mama and Granddaddy would really be proud of me then. That was something for me to think about.

I visited with them until almost nine o'clock. Then I told Ben that I better get back so I could let Alice in and get ready for work the next day. On the way home, he asked me if I needed some money. I would like to have said no. I hated to be a burden on my people. But I only had two dollars of the ten that I got from Alice left.

"Yes, I could use a few dollars and I'll give it back to you when I get paid."

"How much is Alice charging you for staying there?"

"She said that we will split everything right down the middle when I get a job, and now I have one. But I won't know how much she's going to ask me for until I get paid. I already owe her ten dollars. I left my purse on her couch while I took a nap and when I looked in it, my money was gone."

"You shouldn't leave your money lying around. Was there anybody there besides you and her?"

"Just some man who she called Jeff. I didn't see him because I was in her bedroom with the door closed. But I heard them arguing about some money that she owed him."

"That's the man that Jean called me about. She said that Alice is tricking for him. I want you to stay clear of him. Don't even talk to him. I'm going to check on you often until you get out of there."

"I think that they broke up. He called us both a bad name and left."

"Why did he call you a bad name?"

"Alice told him that she couldn't give him the money because she needed it to help me."

When he pulled up to Alice's door and stopped, he took thirty dollars out of his wallet and gave it to me. "Thank you. I'll pay you back as soon as I can."

"Consider it a gift. I'm glad that I can help you. Feel free to call on me anytime."

"Thanks, but I'll be all right after this."

I kissed him on his cheek and got out. "I'll call you soon." I went into the apartment and laid ten dollars on the table for Alice.

When she came home, Jeff was with her. She introduced us and we shook hands. He held my hand an uncomfortably long time, so I pulled it away. He gave me a sly smile and sat down on the couch. I started in the bedroom and Alice asked, "What is this?"

She was looking at the ten dollars on the dinette table. I turned around and said, "It's yours. It's the ten that you loaned me."

"Where did you get money from?"

"Ben gave it to me. I was over there tonight."

"Oh," she said flatly.

I went into the bedroom and pulled the door too. I could still smell Jeff's funny smelling cologne or voodoo potion or whatever it was. The odor was on my hands so I went into the bathroom and washed them. I wondered what Alice saw in him. Not that he was ugly. On the contrary, he was quite handsome. But anybody could tell that he was a fast street man. He even had his hair conked, and his fingernails were long with clear fingernail polish on them.

The odor of his cologne was familiar to me. I had smelled that same odor at Gloria's house. It was intended to captivate and bewitch people. But all that it did to me was made me nauseated.

I actually threw up the time I went to New Orleans with Gloria to get her a mojo hand. She asked Mama to let me go to New Orleans with her to see a doctor about her headaches. But instead, she went to see a sorcerer. We went to New Orleans by bus and then took a taxicab from the bus station to this lady's house. Gloria told me that this lady was a hundred and forty years old. I didn't believe it but Gloria did. On our way to the house, the taxicab driver asked Gloria all kinds of questions about herself and she answered freely. When we got to this woman's house, the driver got out and told us to wait while he went in. Then he came back out and got us. The old lady sent her assistant out to the anteroom to get Gloria and I waited for her there. The assistant kept an eye on me and when I got sick, she showed me to the bathroom.

When Gloria came out, she had a smile on her face and a dab of oil on her forehead. The assistant called us a cab and we went back to the bus station and took the next bus home. That dab of oil and a chance to see a little of New Orleans was all that Gloria got for her money. Nothing changed in her life as a result of that trip. But Gloria believed that it was going to happen any day. She thought that Mr. Right was going to appear out of nowhere.

I heard Jeff and Alice talking and it sounded like they had made up. I set my alarm clock and went to sleep, but not before I tied my money to my bra strap. When the alarm went off the next morning, I shut it off as fast as I could. I didn't want to disturb Alice. But when I looked over on her side of the bed, she wasn't there. I got up and looked out in the living room. She and Jeff were asleep on the couch. I took a bath, got ready and watched out of the window for Gene. Alice was asleep, but Jeff woke up and looked over at me. But I pretended to be looking out of the window and didn't see him. Gene and Bertha finally drove up and I went out of the door quietly and locked it. I spoke to them and got in the back seat. I didn't laugh at Gene this time because it wasn't a shock. He was dressed the same way minus the pumps. This time, he had on flats, and a different tee-shirt.

When we got to the motel, the same woman was on duty. When we walked in, she had a little smirk smile on her face. We walked up to the desk and she spoke and told me where to report to. "But you can't start yet because there's a problem," she said to Gene.

"What kind of problem?"

"We need to have your sex determined."

"My sex determined! What do you mean? My sex was determined before I was born."

She looked over her glasses and said, "Don't toy with me boy because I could have you arrested."

Gene looked at me and said, "Let's go," and we left there in a hurry.

The woman called to me, but I kept going. I didn't want the job unless Gene could work with me. We took the transit bus back to the Westside. Bertha had dropped us off and went on to her job. Gene made me promise not to tell anybody what happened at the motel. He said that he would tell Bertha. It was Friday, so we decided to wait until Monday and look for a job at a laundry. Gene told me to just say that I was eighteen.

That Sunday, I spent the day with Ben and his family, and went to church with them. The Baptist church was a whole lot different from my church back home. It was a whole lot quieter. At our church, we made a whole lot of noise. It was hard to recognize some of the hymns because they sang them so slow and quiet. But I enjoyed the change.

On Monday, Gene got one of his friends to take us to the laundry to see about a job. Gene dressed in his own clothes this time. We both got hired again. I got hired on the presser and Gene got hired sorting linen. It was hot in that laundry and the work was hard too. But my first pay check made me very happy. It was more money than I had ever made at one time. I was paid a dollar an hour and promised a raise in three months if I worked out.

The presser was a whole lot different from using an iron. But I caught on after getting burned a few times. I paid Alice what she asked for and sent ten dollars home to Mama. I kept asking different people if they knew where I could apply for nursing school. Finally one lady gave me all of the details, so I took off one day and applied. She also told me that her niece was a nurse's aide and I could try that too. I thanked her for that information because I could go to school in the day time and work as a nurse's aide at night. She said that she would introduce me to her niece so she could help me. I decided not to tell anybody until I was in. But Alice got the notification out of the mail box and opened it, so I went on and told her that I was taking the test.

CHAPTER XI

Mossy...

I took the bus back to Ellen's apartment. After I had rested for a while, I walked to the neighborhood store and bought food so I could cook her a good meal. When she got home, I told her what had happened. She said she wasn't surprised that my job hadn't worked out.

"After seeing your co-workers when I came to pick you up, I knew you didn't belong there. You're a cut above them."

The thought hadn't crossed my mind because I was just glad to have a job. I hadn't thought about the fact that the women were all big, robust and unattractive. And the men, except Myron, all looked as if they should have been swinging from a tree.

After I lost my job, I was back to cooking and cleaning for Ellen and taking long walks. One day after my walk, I looked in the mailbox and there was a letter addressed to Ellen from Mama. When Ellen started reading it, she got a long face.

"What is it?"

"Mama wants you to come back home."

She started reading the letter out loud. It read, 'Dear Ellen: I received your letter and was very glad to hear from you. I was so happy to hear that Mossy is there with you. I had a feeling that she was with you when night came and she still wasn't home. Your Daddy said that he didn't know what had happened to her because she didn't say nothing to him about leaving. I held off writing to you for a while because I was mad. You shouldn't have kept Mossy there. When she got to you, you should have sent her right back. She needs to be home. She's not ready for that fast life you lead.' And then Ellen stopped reading and frowned.

"What is it?" I asked.

"Aunt Florence and her big mouth! Mama thinks that you're pregnant."

"Let me see that," I said, and took the letter out of her hand. I started reading where she stopped. It read, 'Florence thinks that Mossy is in family way. She says that when a girl just up and runs away, that is usually the case. Ellen, do the right thing and send her home. And don't be taking her to those places that you go to. She's too young for that.' There was nothing else except the closing, so I handed the letter back to Ellen.

"What places is she talking about?"

"I go out sometimes. One time, I saw a man get stabbed to death and I made the mistake of telling her about it."

"I would like to go some place rather than stay closed up in this apartment all the time."

"What are we going to do about you?"

"What do you mean?"

"Mama is not going to let you stay here in no peace. We're going to have to do something. I don't want her mad at me and thinking that I'm upholding you."

"Don't worry about it, I'll write her and mail it tomorrow while I'm on my walk."

"Be sure," Ellen said and we got off the subject.

The next day, I wrote Mama like I said. I wrote, 'Dear Mama, How are you? I'm fine and I hope that you are the same. I want to apologize for leaving home without telling you or anyone else. But I just had to leave. I'm not pregnant and it was nothing that you done neither. I just had to go. I love you very much Mama. I always have, and I always will. I just can't stay in Marlin. I don't feel like it's my home anymore. And Ellen did try to get me to go back, but I told her no. I borrowed forty dollars from your stash in the chifforobe, so I'm enclosing twenty dollars now. And I will send twenty more later. Mama, please don't be mad at Ellen. It is not her fault that I left or that I'm not coming back. I don't know if I'm going to stay here in Dallas neither. I don't like it here. I was talking to a girl the other day on my walk and she's talking about going out West. She said that the jobs are plentiful out there and it's the law that they have to pay you at least one dollar an hour. So, by the time you get this letter, I may be heading west. Give my love to all and please take good care of Betsy and Red for me. I will close for now. Your daughter, Mossy L. Lewis.'

I couldn't bear to call Daddy by name and just so she wouldn't notice the difference, I didn't call Aunt Florence by name neither. I walked down to the mailbox the next day and mailed her letter.

That Friday evening, Ellen came home from work and told me that one of her co-workers was giving a party and we were invited. She told me to try on one of her black dresses to see if it would fit me.

"It will make you look at least five years older and more sophisticated."

I tried it on and lo and behold, it fitted me better than it did her, which made Ellen a tad bit jealous. She dropped down on her couch and said, "Mossy, you've grown into a beautiful, voluptuous young woman."

"Thank you my dear sister."

But I started taking the dress off because I didn't like what I saw in her face. And moreover, she used the term woman. She had never called me a woman before and she didn't like to be called a woman herself. She thought that it made you sound old and matronly. She preferred the word lady, and so did I. I hung the dress back on the hanger and laid it across a chair.

"I would rather for you to wear that one. You can find me something else to wear."

"It does more for you than it does for me, so you can have it if you want it."

"No, you keep it. I don't know where I would wear it to. I can't wear it to church because my armpits would be out."

"You wear it to places like we're going tonight. And I want you to wear it. I want to show off my little sister."

"Thanks Ellen."

She went into her closet, took out a pair of high-heel shoes and sat them down in front of me.

"Try them on."

"Oh no! Please don't make me wear those. I wouldn't be comfortable because they would make me taller than you and I don't like that."

"You're already taller than me."

"I know. But those heels would make me even more so."

"A tall woman is considered graceful. I don't ever want to see you slouching your shoulders, no matter how tall you grow."

"Don't you think I'm through growing? I'm going to be eighteen soon," I said hopefully.

"Maybe. But you might grow as tall as Aunt Mossy. Either way it's all right. I wish that I was you."

That sure meant a lot coming from Ellen because I've always wanted to be her.

I took a bath and dressed while Ellen was curling her hair. I looked at myself in the mirror and hollered, "Wow! Tina Turner don't have nothing on you Mossy."

When Ellen got dressed, I combed her hair out and we left for the party. As soon as we got there, she introduced me around and showed me to a seat on the couch. She brought me a glass of wine and told me to sip it slow.

"It sort of sneaks up on you."

The wine tasted good and I sipped like she said. But since I didn't have anybody to talk to, I was steady sipping. Before I knew it, the glass was empty. The girl sitting next to me said, "I'm about to refill my glass, can I get you another one?"

"Sure, thank you," I answered and handed her my glass. As soon as she got up, a man sat in her seat.

"Excuse me, but that seat is taken, I said politely. The girl will be right back. She just left to get some wine."

"Honey, you must not get out very much," he said in a voice between that of a male and a female. "But around here, when you move, you lose. That's the Mississippi Rule. But I guess that I had better get up from here before I have to read you." He got up and swished away.

This is not fun like Ellen said it would be. I'm making enemies already.

I wanted the girl to sit there so I would have somebody to talk to. I was planning to strike up a conversation as soon as she got back. That first glass of wine had me feeling friendly. I would have liked to have sat with Ellen so we could sip wine and poke fun at people, but Ellen was as wild as all get out. She hadn't sat down since we walked in. And she hadn't paid me no mind since she introduced me around and showed me to my seat.

The girl returned with two glasses of wine and handed one to me. I thanked her and slid over and gestured for her to sit down.

"I'm going to mingle with the crowd. Enjoy yourself."

I thanked her again and started in on my second glass of wine. I drank the second glass a lot faster than I had the first. After I finished it, I got up, walked over to the table and refilled my glass again. I was beginning to feel light headed and the music and the voices were starting to annoy me. I made my way back to my seat and there was a couple sitting there. They looked small and even the couch looked smaller. I looked about the room and everybody looked small. They had all turned into midgets right before my eyes. The couple moved over to let me sit down. But it didn't seem like near enough room. I felt huge like I was about ten feet tall. So I walked over and stood against the wall. After I gulped down that third glass of wine, my knees and elbows began to feel tired. I felt like my feet weren't going to hold me anymore, so I sat down on the arm of the couch. I sat on some woman's arm, and she hollered and moved over. I slid down in the corner of the couch and sat my glass on the floor. I felt pushed so I got back up to find the bathroom. All of the clamoring had gotten on my last nerve and I wanted to fight. I was wishing that one of the midgets would say something that I didn't like so I could slap their face. I tried to find Ellen among them, but I couldn't. So I asked for directions to the bathroom and someone pointed it out. I went in and used the toilet. Then I decided that I didn't want to mingle with the little people anymore. I needed a nap. So I took all of the towels from the rack, spread them out in the bathtub and got in. I pulled the shower curtains too and went to sleep.

Ellen missed me and started looking for me. Some woman told her, "Maybe it's your sister in the bathtub. There are two people in the bathtub with the shower curtain closed, making out. I heard them and I hurried up and got out of there."

Ellen walked into the bathroom and pulled back the curtains. She was relieved to find me asleep in the bathtub alone. One of her friends helped her get me to the car. She took me home and put me to bed.

The next morning, she told me what the person had said and how embarrassed it had made her. "I'm sorry that I ruined your social life," I told her. "But you shouldn't have left me alone. I wouldn't have gotten drunk if I'd had somebody to talk to."

"It's okay. Worst things than that have happened at some of the parties I've been to. One time a man got drunk, whipped it out and started spraying people. I've got to go now or I'll be late for work."

"Have a good day. I'll have your dinner ready when you get off."

"Don't bother. We're going out again tonight. I'm taking you out to eat and then to a bar. I'm going to teach you how to hold your liquor."

"Do I have to?"

"Yes, it will be fun," she said and left.

Now I understood what Mama and Aunt Florence meant about her wild life style. I didn't like it and I didn't like Dallas. Before, I couldn't wait to get to Dallas to be with her. I thought I would be so happy, going shopping, to the movies and out to eat. But Ellen hadn't changed since she was young. She always carried a big crowd. When she lived at home, there were always kids around our house.

I got up and started cleaning up the apartment. While I was cleaning, I ran across some of Ellen's old letters. There were letters from Rachel and Sarah. Rachel lived in Compton, California.

That's where that girl that I'd met was planning to go.

Robert Jr. and Joseph lived there also, but Sarah had moved to Henderson, Nevada. Sarah called Compton nigger town, so I didn't want to go there. I decided that I would write to Sarah and ask her if I could come to Henderson. After cleaning up, I ate breakfast and then wrote to Sarah. When I finished the letter, I took a walk and mailed it. On my way home, I stopped by the store and bought food and cooked. Although Ellen had said don't bother, I knew that she would eat it if it was there.

When she got home from work, we ate, got ready and went out. We went to a small neighborhood bar called

'Clem's Place.' Ellen knew almost everybody there including the owner, Clem. She introduced me to Clem and some of the others. It seemed that they were all regulars and knew each other. Ellen and I sat together at the bar. This time I ordered Coca-Cola. The black dress made me look older than my years, so nobody asked me my age. I was just about to tell Ellen about my decision to go to Nevada to live with Sarah, when some man walked in named Wild Bill. He walked up to the bar and everybody was saying, "Hi Bill."

Clem said, "I missed you Bill. Where have you been?"

"Attending Revival meetings."

Another man laughed and asked, "Did you get religion?"

"I got religion and was baptized over twenty years ago."

The same man asked, "What kind of religion allows you to get drunk every night?"

Clem opened a bottle of beer and sat it in front of Bill. He took a swallow.

"Man if you know what's good for you, you will lay off my religion."

"Fuck you and your religion."

Bill hit the bar with his fist. "I've told you now, my religion is where I draw the fucking line."

A big grisly man came from behind a partition and told the men that they had to settled down or leave. Bill paid for his beer and left. Then the big man said teasingly, "I don't want to hear no more religion or politics tonight." He laughed and went back behind the partition.

I sat there astonished. It never ceased to amaze me how different people think of religion. I had heard some say what they would do to someone if they didn't have religion. And I had heard others say, "I'll lay my religion down and kick your ass." Aunt Florence always says, "Lucky for you that I'm a religious woman." It makes me wonder what they think religion is.

That night was the last time I went out with Ellen. I'd had enough of the Dallas night life and Ellen's friends. From then on, I stayed home and was glad to do so. But I worried about her because it was no telling when something could go wrong. I'd had no idea that she lived that way. She was so level headed when she came home. I wished that I could talk her into going West with me. I was expecting to hear from Sarah in about ten days. I was giving my letter five days to get to her and five days for hers to get back to me. Ellen wasn't disappointed at all when I told her that I was planning to leave Dallas. She thought that it was for the best, so Mama wouldn't be mad at her. While I was waiting for my letter from Sarah, I continued to cook and clean for Ellen.

My calculation was two days off. I received an answer from Sarah on the eighth day. The night before, I'd had a dream about being in this strange place with all these bright lights. I saw a silver dollar lying on the sidewalk. I stooped down to pick it up, but it was stuck to the sidewalk. Then a little girl came along and picked it up. She smiled and handed it to me. When I woke up, I had my hand clinched in a fist. I opened it and expected to see the silver dollar. The dream was so real.

That day, I was coming back from my walk just as the mailman ran. I took the mail out of the box as soon as he put it in there. I fanned through the mail, and when I saw a letter addressed to me from Sarah, I jumped for joy. It said that she would be glad to have me come to Henderson and live with them. She enclosed her telephone number and a money order made out to me for thirty-five dollars.

Two days after I got Sarah's letter, I had my clothes packed and Ellen drove me to the bus station. She waited with me until the bus came. We hugged and kissed, and I asked her again to please think about coming West. "I won't say never," she said, "but it won't be anytime soon. Here in Dallas, I can check on Mama and Daddy, without staying with them."

"Well so long," I said and stepped up on the bus. Then I turned around and hollered "Ellen, I love you."

She hollered, “I love you too baby. Take care of yourself,” and then she was gone.

I found a seat and put my carry on overhead. Then I sat down and leaned back. I thought, *It’s finally over. Except for Mama, Ellen and Aunt Florence, I’m not going to miss Texas at all. I just want this bus to start moving so I can get out of here and leave my hideous past behind me.*

CHAPTER XII

Alice…

Jeff called me and apologized for calling Meredith and me bitches. "I shouldn't have disrespected your sister like that," he said. "I don't even know her." I played along with him knowing perfectly well why he was calling me. It definitely wasn't because he was sorry that he had called us bitches. He wanted the money that I'd held out on him.

"Thank you Jeff. This really means a lot to me."

"So are we tight again?" he asked sounding somewhat sincere.

"I don't know, because that shit really did hurt me. Like you said, you don't even know my sister and she hasn't done a thing to you. So, I want you to prove to me that you're really sorry."

"I told you that I am. What else do I have to do?"

"I thought that you would never ask. I want you to bring me lunch to my job this evening. I take lunch at five o'clock."

"Where am I supposed to get the money from? You reneged on me remember?"

"You're working," I reminded him. "And if I'm not worth lunch, then no, we're not tight."

"What do you want me to bring you?"

The food wasn't important to me, so I said, "I don't know, surprise me. But the main thing is to be there at least five minutes before lunch. And don't wait in your car. Bring the food inside the laundry and wait by the front door."

"Why do I have to do all of that? Are you gonna have some dude waiting inside to clobber me?"

"No silly," I said laughing. "I just wanna know that you're there. I don't buy lunch from the lunch wagon anymore since the food made me sick. I usually catch a ride with somebody to get lunch."

"Okay, I'll scrape up the money from somewhere and bring you a plate."

"Thank you Jeff. I'll see you a little before five o'clock."

I hung up the phone and smiled. I wanted him to come inside so Naomi and those other jealous hearted bitches could see him bringing me lunch. I knew that it would burn Naomi up to see that we were still together. She would rather see Jean with Jeff than me. Gene told me about Jean to warn me. But Naomi tells me about seeing Jeff with her to hurt my feelings. She never once mentioned that Jean walks with a limp. Gene told me. And when I asked her about it, she lied. "I wasn't watching her that close," she said.

When Naomi came to pick me up for work, she wanted to come in to meet Meredith, but I told her that Meredith was job hunting. And just then, Bertha, Meredith and Gene pulled up, so she got to see Meredith anyway. "Your sister is cute."

"Thank you, she took after me." She didn't respond. That shut her up because even without my make-up, I still looked better than her.

Naomi told some of the other women in the laundry about Meredith being here. They were saying that they hope Meredith didn't turn out like me. I caught Naomi in the restroom laughing right along with the others. And she should be the last to talk. Her life was just as fucked up as mine. She had two kids and an old man who wouldn't work. She must have talked to him about me because he tried to trick with me for ten dollars of her money. I didn't dare tell her because she would have just gotten mad at me. Then I would have had to find another ride to work. I didn't pay no attention to what those women around there said about me. The most of them were just ignorant field hands from Louisiana, Mississippi, and Texas.

I thought about telling her that I was having my lunch brought to me, but I decided to keep it under my hat and surprise her. Her eyes were already large and I knew that they would get even larger when she saw Jeff with food for me. At five minutes until five, I looked over at the door and there stood Jeff. He was holding a plate covered with aluminum foil. I waved and he waved back. I cut my eyes at Naomi and she was looking and so were the others who were in sight of the door. I fed the mangle until five o'clock and then walked up to Jeff, took the plate from him and kissed him. After I was satisfied that everybody had seen us together, I told Jeff, "Let's go eat in your car."

He had brought me bar-be-cue ribs, potato salad and baked beans. We sat in his car and ate and talked. He stayed with me through my whole lunch hour. I got tired of his company and kept looking at my watch. If he was not talking about money or a john, he didn't have anything to say. But I stuck it out because I wanted to see how many hints he was gonna throw out before he asked for the money. He told me how much the food cost, and said that it was all he had. Then he cranked up his car and looked at his gas gauge. "I hope I have enough gas to make it back home. It's a long ways out here. If you hadn't reneged on me, I was gonna fill up my tank. Do you still have the money?"

"I have some of it. I bought food with the other."

"Hot links?"

"Food. Meredith knows how to cook."

"Don't you think that I'm entitled to some of it?" he asked sadly.

"Yes, and I might consider giving it to you on one condition."

"I'm afraid to ask what it is, but what is it?"

"Come back tonight at nine o'clock, pick me up and spend the night with me."

He hesitated and then said, "Okay, but how much is left?"

"I don't know. It's at home and I didn't count it."

"Okay, I'll be waiting out here at nine o'clock."

He leaned over for me to kiss him. I gave him a quick peck on his lips and said, "Until tonight," and got out of his car.

When I went back to work, the two women working on the mangle with me started whispering. Then they started feeding the sheets through faster than I could fold them, so I turned the mangle off until I caught up. And I kept cutting it off until they started feeding it right. When it was my turn to feed it, I didn't even try to get even. I knew that they were just jealous.

At nine o'clock, I told Naomi that I was riding home with Jeff. And just to appease her and make sure that I still had a ride to work, I said, "I'll still pay you and I'll see you tomorrow."

Jeff brought me home and I introduced him to Meredith, but she acted all funny. When I found out that she had been to see Ben, I knew why. I didn't feel so good after finding out that she had been with Ben. I wanted Jeff to leave, but I let him stay. We slept out on the couch and made love, but my heart wasn't in it. I knew that he was just there for the money, not because he wanted to be with me. When it was over, I turned my back to him and tried to remember if there was ever a time in my life that I'd been happy for any period of time. I couldn't think of any. The closest I had come to being happy was the time I spent with Nicolas.

Nicolas was this white guy who I met through Jeff. I tricked with him and we got something going that lasted six months. He was from New York and was working in Las Vegas on a contract. He admitted to me that he was living out a fantasy. He told me that he was born in Georgia and he'd always wanted to know what it was like to be with a black woman. But he treated me good, so I didn't care. I was living out a fantasy too. My fantasy was to have a man who catered to my every whim. And I had one, a white one at that. He had his own place, but we were together most of the time when we weren't working. He took me to places like Los Angeles, San Francisco and Phoenix. He always rented a hotel room and sneaked me in. It was so much fun. We made love almost every night.

One night we were making love when his wife called. We stopped and he talked to her for a while. He told her that he loved her and missed her so much that he didn't know what to do. She must have said that she loved him too because he said, "I love you more. Kiss the kids for me." Then he hung up and we finished making love.

I didn't take it too hard when his contract was over and he went back to his wife and kids. By then, I was about ready to come back down to earth anyway. Before he left, he made me promise that I would stay away from prostitution and Jeff. I said that I would and made him promise to write to me. I was at the mailbox every day looking for a letter that never came. He didn't keep his promise and neither did I.

One day while I was at the mailbox, Jeff passed by and I hailed him down. He marveled at how well I looked. He came by my apartment that night and we made love. It wasn't long before we were talking on a regular basis again. And as soon as the work started slowing down at the laundry, I let him talk me into the same old shit. I had wanted to see Jean and Blanche when I was with Nicolas, but I never ran into neither one of them. Now here I was back to dodging them again.

The next morning, I went on and gave Jeff twenty dollars because I didn't feel like fighting with him. He took it and said that he would be back that night. But I knew that he wouldn't, and I didn't care. I decided to spend more time with Meredith so she wouldn't leave me for Ben. I let her talk me into going downtown to shop and we were just about to walk into an expensive store when I ran smack dab into Blanche. It was the first time I had seen her in years. I had even stopped going to the church we used to attend to avoid seeing her. I pretended not to see her, but she said, "Hi Alice. Long time no see."

"Oh hi Blanche, I didn't see you," I lied. "We're in kinda a hurry."

She looked at Meredith and asked, "Is this your sister?"

"Yes it is. I'll see you."

I walked into the store behind Meredith. She followed us into the store and asked, "What's the big rush? Do you have a hot date? By the way, how are tricks? And where do you hang out? Jean has been looking for you."

I stopped and told Meredith to go ahead and look around. As soon as she was out of earshot, I asked Blanche, "What does Jean wanna see me about? She must not have been looking too hard for me. I've been right here in Vegas, except for the times when I went out of town with Nicolas."

"Who is Nicolas?"

"Oh, you don't know him. I met him after I moved."

"Well that is not what I heard. I heard that you're fucking Jeff and turning tricks for him."

"Oh you did?"

"Yes I did. And that is some cold shit because I thought we were all supposed to be friends. You didn't even tell the truth about where you were moving too. Jeff was why you moved so fast, wasn't he?"

"No he wasn't. I moved because I wanted a place of my own and a comfortable bed to sleep in. How do you think I felt having to wait until your company left, so I could go to bed?"

"It was better than what you had. Your brother put your ass out in the streets, and now I can see why. But like I told you, Jean is the wrong person to fuck with."

A white man who worked in the store had started hanging around so I didn't answer her last remark. I tried to walk away, but she hollered, "Jean is gonna get your ass."

I turned around and walked back up to her. I squinted my eyes and looked dead into hers, hoping to intimidate her. But she stared right back into mine and said, "Jean is my friend. And I don't like what you done. Just in case you wanna know what happened to the money you gave Jeff, he used it to pay her portion of the rent while she was laid up."

I didn't believe that, but it made me mad just the same. So I said, "I don't give a fuck what he gave her. And she can have the no account, two-timing son-of-a-bitch. I don't want him because he ain't gonna never amount to a hill of beans."

She knew that was the truth, so she couldn't think of a comeback. I walked away fast and she hollered, "Watch out for Jean." Then she laughed and walked out of the store.

I was so mad, that I was shaking. I found Meredith and took it out on her. "Who was that girl? She didn't act too friendly."

"It was just some old somebody that I used to know."

She held up a pair of lace nylon panties and asked, "What do you think about these? They cost five dollars a pair."

"They're just draws Meredith. What am I supposed to think about them? Why do you need expensive draws? Nobody is gonna see them but you." Then I mumbled under my breath, "With your no fucking self."

But I wanted her to spend her money, so she wouldn't be saving it up, so I said, "Buy the damn things and let's go."

"Oh I can get them later, if you're in a hurry." She folded them nicely and put them down.

"Then let's get the hell out of here." I didn't want to give Blanche enough time to go get Jean.

We left and made it to the bus stop just in time to catch the Westside bus. As soon as we got on the bus, Meredith started yakking. It took all that I could do to keep from telling her to shut the fuck up. But I just folded my arms and closed my eyes. She caught the hint and stopped talking. And then I could think. *I'm glad that I was smart enough not to give Jeff everything.*

I had even been smart enough to build up my own small clientele. I collected telephone numbers from dates that he had gotten for me, and then called them on my own. I had out smarted Jeff in every way. *He is just a wanna be pimp. I just want him to call me or come by so we can have a real show down. Then I'll keep him out of my life for good. I wish I had never met Jeff, Jean or Blanche. Now I have to watch out for that crazy ass Jean for the rest of my life. I should leave Las Vegas and move to Los Angeles. I could try to get a job in an art studio. But with my luck, I would probably end up on skid row. Maybe when I get Jeff out of my life, this will blow over. He will find somebody else to cheat with and Jean will forget about me and get after her. I envy Meredith's simple life.*

When we got off the bus on the Westside, I started walking fast to get to my apartment. I just wanted to get inside and out of danger. No sooner than we got inside the apartment, somebody knocked on the door. I screamed at Meredith, "Don't open that door." She looked at me so strange that I felt embarrassed. "Always look through the window and see who it is first."

She looked through the curtain and said, "It's Gene. Can I let him in?"

"Yes." I went into the bedroom and sat on the bed. My hands were shaking uncontrollably. I really thought that Blanche and Jean had followed me home.

Gene and his new boyfriend had come by to invite Meredith to the Convention Center. They were going to see some singing group. Before he left, he came into the bedroom and asked if I wanted to go. I told him no. But I did want to go, I was just afraid that Jean and Blanche might be there. I knew that Jeff wouldn't be there because he didn't spend money on social events.

Except for going to work, I stayed close to home for the next couple of weeks. Jeff didn't call or come by. That's how I knew that he had heard about the altercation between Blanche and me. It was way past the time for me to get my hair done. I'd broken two appointments with Beulah because I was afraid to go up on the Set. Finally, I couldn't stand my hair any longer. My red streak was black and red. So I called Beulah to make another appointment. The only opening she had was on a Friday morning. Something bothered me about that day and I almost turned it down, but I didn't want to make Beulah mad so I took it.

By the time Friday rolled around I was so desperate to have my hair done that I just ignored the uneasy feeling I had. When I got to the shop, all of the operators were busy and about three people were waiting. Beulah was talking about some beautician who was drunk. The beautician had solicited a customer from the street outside of the shop and burned most of the girl's hair off. They were all laughing at Beulah's story. One of the operators said that she was winking her eyes and shaking her head, trying to give the girl a hint. But the girl didn't catch it, so she gave up.

Beulah put her customer under the dryer and called me. I sat in her chair and she draped me with a plastic cape. "I want my streak a little wider. And I would like you to make it a little lighter."

"I think you should let me condition this hair before I put any more chemicals on it. It's too brittle, it will break."

"Can't you give me the streak and conditioner too?"

"I can give you anything you want. I just want you to know that this patch is weak and may fall out."

I didn't answer her so she handed me the comb and said, "Show me how wide you want it."

I parted off a section of my hair and handed the comb back to her. Beulah said to the operator next to her, "Now you're my witness that I told her." And the operator just smiled.

"I like color in my hair. If I don't have but three strands, I want one of them red." I liked my streak because several men had told me that it made me look exotic.

Beulah clamped my hair off and started putting the chemicals on it, against her will. I knew that what she was saying was right, but I had to have my streak. It was a part of me now. I would just have to take good care of it so it wouldn't fall out. For one thing, I wasn't going to comb it much. Beulah asked out loud, "Why is it that when a woman gets hell in her, or is in a bad mood, she takes it out on her hair? Why don't they just go and buy a hat? That's what I do when I'm in a bad mood, I go hat shopping."

"Then you must have a room full of hats," another operator said.

"Girl, I ain't got you up," Beulah said and they all laughed. Just then Jean walked through the front door. I started sliding down in the chair.

"Girl, what is wrong with you? I haven't even finished putting this stuff in your hair yet, so I know it can't be burning you."

"I need to use the restroom bad."

"Well why didn't you say so." She backed away and let me up.

The restroom was right by the back door. I went in, took the plastic cape off and threw it on the restroom sink. Then I came out and kept straight out of the back door. I left my purse at Beulah's station. She ran to the back door and yelled, "Alice," but I kept running.

There was a vacant lot out back where they had torn down a building. I ran across rocks and broken glass until I reached the street. Then I flagged down the first car that passed. An old man stopped and gave me a ride. He looked at my hair strange but he didn't' say anything. "Where are you heading?"

I gave him my address. Then I thought about not being able to get in unless I went to the office because Meredith wasn't home. I needed to get that shit out of my hair, it had started heating up. So I told the old man, "Take me to my sister's house on Van Buren," and I gave him Bertha's address. Her house was a lot closer than my apartment.

When we got to Bertha and Johnnie's house, I jumped out, thanked him and apologized for not being able to give him something for his gas. But he said that he didn't want anything anyway and looked up at my hair again. After he drove off, I knocked on Bertha's door, knowing that they weren't home. Then I grabbed the water hose and started washing my hair. Gene came from around the side of the house and said, "Alice, what are you doing?"

"What does it look like I'm doing?" I squeezed the water out of my hair and wiped my face with my hand. "I'm washing my hair."

"But why here?"

I couldn't think of a good answer. "Why don't you mind your own business?"

"Oh now that's a knee slapper. You're in my front yard washing your head with my water hose and I should mind my own business."

I turned the water hose off. "Gene, I really need your help."

"Okay. What is it you need me to do?"

"Jean came in the beauty shop while I was there. I heard that she's carrying a gun for me, so I left. But I left my purse at Beulah's station. And I need you to go and get it for me."

"Okay, but you should leave Jeff alone. He's not worth you getting killed about. Let Jean have him."

"Well I plan to after this. But he's been lying and saying that he wasn't having nothing to do with her. And you should hear how bad he talks about her."

"Well I told you that I saw them together. So you believed him over me?"

"I don't wanna get into that now."

"This is your own fault."

"I believe you now. And it won't happen again, I promise. Please just go ahead and get my purse."

"Okay, but come in and call Beulah and tell her that I'm picking it up."

I dialed the beauty shop and Beulah picked up on the first ring. "This is Alice."

Beulah hollered, "Alice, where are you?"

"I'm at my cousin's house."

"Wash that stuff out of your hair right away."

"I did."

"I found out why you left. Jean started talking about you to another customer. But she wasn't after you. She had an appointment with Frances. Jean knows better than to start anything up in here. Come on back so I can put a conditioner on that hair."

"I'm too ashamed Beulah. Put me down for tomorrow please."

"Okay. I'll work you in, but be here around eight tomorrow morning."

"Thanks Beulah. And Gene will be there in a few minutes to get my purse. Is Jean still in there?"

"Yes."

"Can she hear you?"

"No, she's up front under the dryer and I'm in the back."

"Okay, I'll see you tomorrow morning." I hung up the phone.

Gene left to get my purse and I washed my hair again with Bertha's shampoo. When Gene got back with my purse, I thanked him and asked him not to tell anybody about what had happened. He promised not to, but I knew that he was gonna tell. It would kill him not to tell. I called a taxicab and went home. I missed another day of work, knowing that I was pressing my luck.

The next morning, I went back to the beauty shop and got my hair done. Nobody mentioned what had happened, and Beulah didn't talk about it neither. It was Saturday and they were rushing around like crazy. I tipped Beulah five dollars because it was gonna be my last time there. Of course I didn't tell her that, but I couldn't take no chance of meeting up with Jean. She had started coming to Beulah's because she knew that I got my hair done there.

Ben took me to Beulah's to get my hair done shortly after I got to Las Vegas. And I had been coming to her ever since. Blanche must have just remembered it after she saw me again. I wasn't a big enough fool to think that Beulah was gonna try to protect me. She's messy herself and she loves to have something to talk about. If Jean had got after me Beulah would have said, "You all take that shit outside." I knew her well after going to her for four years. I had to give up my beautician, but at least I got to see for myself that Jean did have a limp.

It was a month before Jeff called me. And he didn't mention anything about the run-in that I had with Blanche. I knew good and well that he'd heard about it. He thought that he'd given me time enough to forget about it. *It's funny how some people think that a little time will erase everything. They think that they can do you something and then give you a little time and you'll forget about the shit. Then they can come back and sock it to you all over again. But not me, I have a memory like an elephant.*

I remembered every word that Blanche said to me and how bad it made me feel. So when he called, I tried to make him feel just as bad as I felt. I listened to him for a while before I socked it to him.

"What have you been doing?" he asked.

"Oh nothing much. What about you?"

"I've been working double shifts trying to pay off my bills so I can blow this dusty town. Just like I told you."

"You've been saying that for over three years now. You know good and well that you ain't going nowhere that you can't gamble."

"Well if you don't believe I'm leaving, you just count the days I'm gone."

"This conversation ain't going nowhere. And I'm losing my patience. So why did you call Jeff? What do you want?"

"I wanna see you."

Deep down inside, I wanted to see him too. But I had to be strong. His actions had caused me a lot of pain and now it was my turn to give him some pain too. So I sneered, "I don't wanna see your no account, lying, two-timing ass no more." And then I added, "You're a low down, scum sucking double zero fly and stay the fuck out of my life." Before he could say anything, I slammed the receiver down. He called right back, but I didn't answer.

After a couple of days passed and he still hadn't called back or come by, I got worried. I hadn't figured on him giving up that easy. But I wasn't about to call him and go crawling back. One thing that I learned from Jeff is that you couldn't buy love.

CHAPTER XIII

Meredith…

Alice claimed that she had broken up with Jeff for good this time. I would be happy except that she was focusing too much of her attention on me. I received a letter from Mama and she opened it.

"I read your letter. I hope you don't mind. I wouldn't have opened it if it had been from a boy or something. But since it was from Mama, I wanted to hear what she had to say."

She looked so depressed that I felt sorry for her. "I don't mind. But you could write to Mama and Gloria and they would write you back. Since you see how good it feels to get mail, why don't you at least write Gloria? She's waiting to hear from you. I just mailed her a letter yesterday."

"I'm gonna write her. I promise. Read your letter out loud, I wanna hear it again."

And so I read it. It read, 'Dear Meredith, I received your letter and the money and thank you very much. We're all fine and your granddaddy sends his love. Baby you missed it last Sunday. The pastor baptized a new member and Sister Carrie's little girl, Mildred. And the thing that I've been telling you all about happened. Do you remember me telling you all that Sister Simms was just putting on, pretending that she was going to run into the river when the pastor is baptizing? Well this past Sunday, the deacons and ushers got together and played a joke on her. They called her bluff. She got to shouting and took off to the river and they just let her go. When she got to the bank and saw that they weren't going to stop her, she fainted at the bank.'

Alice and I laughed and I stopped reading the letter. We started talking about old times and she said, "I told you too that Sister Simms wasn't gonna take her dressed up ass into that river. Don't you remember me telling you that when we were little?"

I didn't remember her ever telling me that, but I said yes anyway. I didn't want to break her upbeat spirit. Mama's letter really perked her up. "That letter reminds me of all the devilment we used to get into in church. Do you remember when I use to pay you all to shout, just to get Sister Simms started?"

I did remember that and I readily agreed. Sister Simms was our church's habitual shouter. She shouted on cue. All she needed to hear was "Hallelujah" or "Praise the Lord" to get her started.

When we were growing up, we attended church eight miles out in the country. It was a small congregation, so it was hard to keep a regular pastor. It seemed that our small church was where a would-be minister came to try out and then went on to a larger church. So the bishop had to send us a visiting minister, but he only came every third Sunday. Every third Sunday, the parents packed baskets of food and we stayed at church all day. The river baptizing was also done on that Sunday. When the morning services were over, the adults put the food out on tables and benches and we ate. Then they cleaned up and visited with the minister and each other while the children played outside. That was when Alice got her congregation ready for the evening services.

She never had any friends of her own because of her abrasive disposition. So, she always played with me and my friends and bossed us around. She told each one of us what to do, some had to shout and some had to testify. She always paid us with candy and bubble gum. We were such good actors that the adults thought we were sincere. To my knowledge, they never did catch on. They were so glad to see us participating in the services that they never realized that Alice was conducting her own service right under their noses.

There was a little boy named Sage who stuttered so bad that he had to hit himself sometimes to get his words out. But one Sunday, he was the only one who agreed to testify. So Alice gave him some candy and told him that she would signal to him when to stand up during the evening service. When she signaled to him, he stood up but he started stuttering and didn't get out a word before somebody led off with another song. I remember laughing until I cried that evening.

Mama's letter brought back a lot of old memories. Alice and I sat and talked and laughed for a long time. It was nice to see her laughing again. I knew what was bothering her, but she didn't know that I knew. Ben had told me. All at once, she burst out laughing and I asked, "What are you laughing about now?"

"I just thought about that time when I got into trouble because you got your face and hair singed."

"How well do I remember that. My hair is still thin in the front."

"And I still have the scar on my thigh from Uncle Major's belt buckle. She showed me a small scar.

"I'm sorry. But, I wanted to see what was happening."

I was six and she was ten when that happened. Mama took us out in the country to see Uncle Major, Aunt Nell and our cousins. Our cousins took us out behind the barn to pick cherry tomatoes, but there were big green tomato worms on the vines. So Alice came up with the idea that the worms should be punished for eating up the tomatoes.

"I know what we'll do," she said. "We'll send them to hell and let them burn from fire and brimstone."

She sent our cousin Elijah to get some matches. First they tried burning the worms right off the vines, but Alice burned her finger and that made her mad.

"Now I'm really mad. Let's knock them off the vines and burn them all together."

One of the boys came up with the idea to get my uncle's oil pan that he used to drain old oil from his truck and tractor. They put the worms in the oil pan and got the gasoline can and poured some on the worms. Alice had the matches. When everything was ready, she hollered, "Everybody get back."

Then she struck a match and threw it into the pan. Everybody jumped back but me. I leaned forward and the blaze jumped up and singed my face and front hair. One of our cousins ran into the house and told that I had gotten burned. Mama, Uncle Major, and Aunt Nell came running. Uncle Major put the fire out and asked his oldest son Elijah to tell him what happened. When he found out, he took his belt off and whipped Alice and Elijah. I can still remember the look on Mama's face when he was whipping Alice. She looked like she was feeling each lash herself. She grabbed his arm and said, "That's enough Major."

We went into the house and she greased my face with tallow. After that, we left and that was the last time she took us out to Uncle Major's house.

She used to say that she believed that Alice was given to her to test her endurance. She never said so, but I think that it really pulled at her heart string when Alice left and never wrote once. I know that it used to hurt me when Mama would say, "There's the mailman. Run see what we got. Maybe we'll have a word from Alice today."

But there was never anything. After months passed and she didn't write, Mama never mentioned hearing from her again. We inquired about her through Gloria. I was angry at Alice, so I never tried to contact her myself. I wasn't angry because she didn't write me. I was angry because it was disrespectful to our grandparents for her not to write them.

When our daddy left us, they took us in and kept us because they loved us. We had aunts and uncles who lived on farms and they wanted us too. But they wanted to work us and probably would have beat the hell out of us. They were always saying that Mama and Granddaddy were too old to be worrying with us and they should let them have us. Whenever Alice acted up, one of my aunts or uncles would say, "I told you that you and Daddy didn't need this trouble. That gal is gonna drive you all to an early grave."

Mama would just say, "I'm doing what Lizza would want me to do. I know that she's somewhere smiling down at me."

When Alice and I finished talking, I answered Mama's letter. I told her that I read her letter to Alice and we laughed about Sister Simms. I also told her that Alice said that she's really going to write to her and Gloria. I was hoping that Alice would keep her word, so I even laid my stationery out to make it handy for her to write.

Alice had been a bundle of nerves ever since we went downtown that day. This angry looking girl insisted on talking to her so she told me to go look around. When she got to where I was, she was trembling. From then on, she jumped every time somebody knocked on the door or the telephone rang. I found out who the girl was from Ben. She was Jeff's old lady Jean's friend. After Jean's friend saw us downtown, she told Jean and Jean called Ben. She told Ben what she was going to do to Alice when she caught up with her. But Ben showed her that blood is thicker than water. He said he told her that if she laid a finger on Alice, she better be ready to deal with him. I'm not supposed to tell Alice because Ben wants her to stay scared so she will stay out of the streets.

For a while, she did stay close to home. When she wasn't working, she moped around and slept a lot. Then one night we were watching television and she jumped up and said, "Shit on this."

She got ready, called a taxicab and went out. She didn't get home until the wee hours of the morning. From then on, she was out every night except when her period was on. During that time, she cursed like the dickens and said men should have periods not women. I was so afraid for her during that time. I would be so glad when I heard her key in the door. Then one night she came in and I could tell that she was in pain. I peeped at her and then pretended to be asleep. A day or so later, I heard her on the telephone telling somebody that she got her ass beat. And then she laughed; it was crazy. It seemed like she thought that she needed punishing and was glad that she had finally gotten it. She didn't seem mad at the person who beat her.

I cooked for her and helped her out, but then she started acting like I was her maid. I finally got tired of it and told her, "I'm going to see Ben."

"But I need you."

"What do you need me for? I've cooked and cleaned up."

"I need company to keep my mind off things," she said sadly.

I stayed with her because being with her or being with Ben's children wasn't that much different. It was like being between a rock and a hard place. Ben and Laura had the worst two children in the world. They didn't even try to discipline them. They just fed them and let them grow. I used to hear that phrase all the time, but I had to meet Lucy and Joyce to appreciate the true meaning of it. Ben told me that Joyce got expelled for being a bad influence on the other children. She was teaching them how to play the dozens and hit one little girl because she couldn't get it right. The little girl told the sisters and Joyce got suspended. Next, she was caught by a sister cursing up a storm and got suspended again. But they finally expelled her when they caught her describing the birth of her puppies. Joyce had a group of the third graders standing right under the window of the school. She told them, "You all should have been at my house and seen my dog. Puppies were falling out of her pussy." Ben and Laura couldn't deny it because their dog had just had puppies.

After Joyce got expelled, they pulled Lucy out too and put them in another private school. Even Laura's freeloading brother couldn't stand to be around the girls for long. He had tried to stay with them, but the girls' bad behavior helped him see the wrong in his ways. He quickly got a job and moved into his own place. Ben not asking me to live with them was a blessing in disguise. We would have ended up like Alice and him, not talking to each other. But now, he was in my corner all the way. He and Gene were the only family members who gave me encouragement about trying to better myself.

Ben was taking me to the test site to take the LPN test. I didn't even talk to Laura about it after the way she snapped Corrine up and Alice was totally against it. She said that I didn't look like the nurse type, and if I did get my foot in the door at all, I'd just end up on a geriatric ward washing some old man's gizzards. Gene was glad that I was trying to get into the hospital because he was planning to work there too. His friend Joel was an orderly and he was always talking about what went on around the hospital.

He told us a story about another orderly named Lamont, who worked with him. He said that Lamont picked up his duty list and it said for him to ambulate one of his male patients. He didn't know what the word ambulate meant and was too embarrassed to ask. So he tried to get Joel to tell him what he was supposed to do for the patient without coming out and asking him. Joel was in the utility room washing urinals and bedpans when Lamont walked in and started a conversation about something trivial. Then he told Joel, "I've got to go because I have to ambulate a patient."

"Okay. I'll catch you later man."

Lamont took a few steps and then turned around and asked, "Man, have you ever had to do anything like that?"

Joel hadn't caught on yet, so he answered, "Yes, I've had to ambulate patients."

"Well, how did it go?"

Now Joel was catching on and it was all that he could do to keep from laughing. But he wanted to play with him awhile longer before he told him, so he said, "Man the last time I had to do it, it was tough."

"But you got it done didn't you?"

"Yes, I got it done."

"Well I'd better get on down there and get it done. You know these kinds of things have to be done."

"Yes I think you had better go and get that patient up and walk him."

Lamont let out a sigh of relief and said, "Thanks a lot man."

"Hold up. I'll go and help you." He showed Lamont how to walk the patient.

I didn't know what ambulate meant neither, but I laughed right along with them and they never knew the difference. After listening to Joel, talk about things that went on around the hospital, I was anxious to get started.

CHAPTER XIV

Mossy...

My travel to Nevada was so enjoyable that I was sorry when it ended. But I couldn't have hoped for a warmer reception than what I received from Sarah and her family. She, her husband, and daughter were eagerly awaiting my arrival. When I stepped off the bus, Sarah started laughing. She grabbed me, hugged me and rocked me from side to side. Sarah has always been very emotional. She was easy to laugh and easy to cry. Her husband Sam stood near by holding their daughter Kim and smiling. He had a striking resemblance to Daddy, which made me uncomfortable. Sarah turned me aloose and asked, "Ain't she pretty?"

"Yes she is, the two of you look alike," Sam answered.

"I don't feel so pretty, but thanks anyway."

"This is Sam and Kim."

"Welcome," Sam said and extended his hand.

I shook his hand and said, "Thank you, I'm glad to be here."

"Hi Aunt Mossy," Kim said, smiling.

"Hi Kim," I said reaching for her.

She leaned forward and I took her from Sam's arm. She was a little butterball and she was much heavier than I expected.

"You're heavy Kim. What do you eat?"

She put her little chubby hand over her mouth and laughed. "If you ate as much grits and bacon as Kim eats, you'd be heavy too," Sarah said.

"Here, I'll take her," Sam said, reaching for her.

"No, I want to get down," she hollered and I let her down.

Sam got my luggage and I picked up my carry-on luggage and we got into the car. Kim sat on the back seat with me. She found her handkerchief that had a silver dollar tied up in it and started swinging it around and talking. She told me about her Persian cat named Boo-Boo Kitty and her dog named Ho-Bo that died. She told me that they buried him in the back yard and promised to show me where he was. "Who named him Ho-Bo?" I asked.

"Daddy did. Somebody put him out and me and Daddy found him sitting beside the road waiting for a ride."

Sarah asked, "How was your trip out here?"

"Great. The only part that I didn't like was changing buses."

"I'm talking to Aunt Mossy."

"Well ex-c-u-se me," Sarah replied.

"Aunt Mossy, my friend has a talking bird. And I asked my daddy to get me one and he's thinking about it." Then she leaned forward and asked Sam, "Daddy are you still thinking about my talking bird?"

"Yes baby, I'm still thinking."

I was sitting behind Sarah and I had a good view of Sam. Even from behind, he favored Daddy. "Sarah, don't you think Sam favors Daddy?"

"A little. Maybe that's why people are always saying that Sam and me favor."

To get my attention back, Kim handed me the handkerchief with the silver dollar tied up in it. "Here Aunt Mossy, this is for you."

Sarah looked back to see what Kim was giving me. I took the handkerchief and started trying to untie the knot. It was so hard. I had to use my teeth to get it untied. I looked at the silver dollar and thought about the dream that I had before I left Dallas. In my dream, the dollar was stuck to the ground. And in real life, I had a hard time getting it untied. Kim must have been the little girl in the dream. I looked at the dollar and said, "Thank you Kim." Then I hugged her. "You're just too adorable. How old is Kim?"

"I'm four years old," Kim yelled out.

"That's right, she's four," Sarah said.

"What are you going to buy with your dollar?" Kim asked. I hugged her again and said, "I'm going to buy candy for you and me. Here, you hold onto our money."

I tied the dollar back up and gave it to her. She took it and said, "I won't lose it," and started bouncing up and down on the seat. Then she started talking about something else. She talked all the way to their house.

Sarah and Sam had a large nice house and nice things in it. They had four bedrooms just like we had in Texas. But our bedrooms were larger because Daddy and two of his brothers built our house. Sarah had me a room fixed up right next to Kim's room. She showed me to my room and Sam brought my luggage in. "That bed looks so good. I feel like I could get in it and sleep for a week," I said.

"Let me show you the rest of the house," Sarah said. "Then I'll fix you something to eat and you can get washed up and take a nap."

"I'm not hungry. But I'll take something cold to drink. Then I want to take a bath and go to bed."

"Can I take a nap with you?" Kim asked.

"No you cannot," Sarah said. "You just want to get in the bed with Aunt Mossy and talk her head off."

The three of us walked from room to room and then went out on the patio. When we came back through the kitchen, Sarah gave me a soda and I gave Kim some of it. Then I went to my room and took out some clothes. I took a bath and lay down. Sarah closed the door to my bedroom to keep Kim out. Before I fell asleep, I could hear Kim playing outside of my bedroom door. I went to the door and told her, "I'm going to take a nap and then get up and play with you."

"Okay," she said excitedly.

But I fell asleep and slept, and slept, and slept. Kim woke me up yelling, "No! No! I don't want to go. I'm waiting for Aunt Mossy. She's fixing to get up and play with me. And I can't be gone. Leave me alone."

"There is no need to be rude young lady," Sarah said. "If you ride with me to get some ice cream for dinner, maybe she will be up when we get back."

"Well all right," Kim consented.

"Then put your shoes back on."

"But I can't buckle they," Kim whined.

"Just put they on and I'll buckle they," Sarah replied. I laughed at the way she humored Kim. One minute Kim sounded like a little old lady, and the next minute she was whining and talking baby talk. They left and I dozed back off.

When they got back, Kim ran into my room and told me, "We bought ice cream and pie. Come on and see."

"Okay, I'll be right there."

I got dressed and went into the kitchen where Sarah was preparing dinner. Kim pointed to the Rhubarb pie on the kitchen counter and told me to look. "Be quiet," Sarah told her. "I need to talk to Aunt Mossy."

Oh no I thought. Now Mama is telling her to send me home. I sat down at the table and asked, "What do you want to talk to me about?"

"What do you think about being a nurse?"

"I think that's great. I've told everybody that you're a Registered Nurse."

“Thank you. But I’m talking about you being a Licensed Practical Nurse. They call them a LPN.”

“I don’t know. I haven’t thought about it. Why?”

“I took the liberty of signing you up. You’re supposed to take the test next Monday morning at eight o’clock.”

“That doesn’t give me much time to study for it.”

“It’s not that hard. I took it myself. I was a LPN for a year before I went to college to be a RN. You just got out of school and your mind is still alert. So this is the time to take it.”

“How did you get me signed up? I thought that I’d have to do that myself.”

“Not if you know the ropes. I got my friend’s daughter Hattie to sign you up. She’s taking the test too. I was just praying that you got here in time. Hattie is tall like you. Actually, she’s taller than you. After she signed herself up, she went back and pretended to be you and it worked. She signed you up without a problem.”

“I probably would have given myself away.”

“Oh that’s common around here. I know a twenty year old girl who went down and took the driving test for her forty-seven year old aunt. She just put on a wig and an oversized dress. Her aunt wore glasses, so she wore a pair of fake eye glasses. She passed the driving test and got her aunt’s license too.”

“That was great. I guess I could pretend to be somebody else if I had to.”

“Sam did it. Hattie’s daddy John had to be out of town on business on the day that he was supposed to take his driving test. So Sam agreed to take it for him. I went with Sam and it’s a good thing that I did. While we were sitting up there waiting for Sam to be called, he started daydreaming. And when the driving examiner called John Allen, Sam had forgotten that he was supposed to be him. After he called for John Allen the second time, I hunched Sam. “That’s you,” I whispered to Sam and he jumped straight up.

"That's me! I'm John Allen."

"Let's go," the examiner said. "You don't act like you've been using that name long."

"Oh yes Sir, that's me. My wife had me distracted."

"Did Sam pass the test?"

"Barely. But he was a nervous wreck. Sam doesn't believe in stepping outside of the law. I talked him into it because John would have done the same thing for him. John and Ruth are our closest friends. You'll meet them when I take you to meet Hattie."

"When?"

"Maybe tomorrow evening."

I got up and helped her set the table. And we got ready and sat down to dinner as they called it. Back home, the evening meal was supper. During dinner, Sam passed the bowl of green beans to me and I dropped the bowl and spilled the beans on the table. Sam was making me nervous already. Sarah saw that I was embarrassed and she said, "You're just like me. I drop almost everything I pick up. There's plenty more on the stove."

I got up to clean the beans off the table and knocked my glass of ice tea over. Kim burst out laughing and Sarah told her to be quiet. "Aunt Mossy is just tired from her trip," she said.

Sarah got up and scooped the beans back into the bowl and put more on the table. I was extra careful for the rest of the evening. And I made it through dinner without anymore spills.

After dinner, Sam left the kitchen and took Kim with him. I felt much better with just me and Sarah alone. I washed the dishes and she dried them and put them away.

"I took a week off to get you settled in. Tomorrow after I drop Kim off at preschool, we'll ride around."

"How far is the Strip from here? I've heard so much about 'The Las Vegas Strip,' I want to see it."

"It's not that far. We're about fifteen miles from Las Vegas. I'll take you there first."

"How old is Hattie?"

"She's your age, maybe a couple of months older. She turned eighteen in June."

"What is she like?"

"What do you mean?"

"I mean is she friendly or stuck up?"

"Both. She's not the same way all of the time. Sometimes she's overfriendly and other times she doesn't want to be bothered. John and Ruth bought her a brand new Ford Falcon for graduation, so you might think that she's a little spoiled."

I felt jealous already, but I smiled to cover it up. "That's good. That's what I'm going to do, save up and get me a car."

"Sam and I will help you get a little car."

"Oh I don't need it now. I don't even know how to drive. I'm too afraid of wrecking."

"There's enough desert out there for you to learn to drive without wrecking. Sam and I will teach you."

I didn't answer, but I wasn't about to let Sam teach me nothing. He looked too much like Daddy for me. Sarah and I hadn't had but one good conversation but I was already tired to death of hearing Sam and I. *Why couldn't she just say that she would do it?*

After we finished cleaning up the kitchen, she brought out a box of puzzles. Boo-Boo Kitty came in meowing, so she fed him. "Hattie gave Sam and me these puzzles for Christmas. We never opened them; but I thought that this would be something that we could all do together. Unless you have something else in mind."

"The puzzle is fine."

She opened the five hundred pieces puzzle and called Sam and Kim into the kitchen. I was already seated, so Kim pushed her chair up close to mine.

"If you're going to sit with Aunt Mossy, you can't start talking. Because Aunt Mossy needs to concentrate."

She showed Kim the picture of the puzzle. "See, we're fixing to build this."

"Can I ask just one question?" Kim asked.

"Just one. And this time I mean it Kim."

"Aunt Mossy do you want to go with me to get my talking bird when my daddy gets through thinking about it?"

I put my arm around her. "That is a loaded question Kim. And I need to think about it."

"That was a very smart answer," Sarah said. We laughed, all except Kim. She didn't understand my answer, but it wasn't what she wanted to hear.

Piecing the puzzle together was more fun than I thought. Kim soon lost interest and left to play with her cat. Sarah got up from the table and asked, "Who wants something to drink?"

"Beer for me," Sam answered.

"Nothing for me," I answered. "I'm still as full as a tick."

Sam cut his eyes at me and kept on with the puzzle. Sarah pretended to ignore it. I was sorry that I'd said it, but it just slipped out. It was a nervous reaction. I knew Sarah had picked up on it because Daddy used to say it all the time. And Sarah was always the one who hollered, "Yuck!"

We all got tired of the puzzle and Sarah put it away. She and Sam went to the family room and I went to Kim's room and played with her. I asked Kim, "Do you like Hattie?"

"Sometimes. She hardly ever plays with me. She calls me a brat and tells me to get away from her. But sometimes she lets me play with her dolls, if I promise not to say another word to her."

Sarah came in and told Kim that it was bed time. So I went to my room and watched television and then went to bed.

It was almost noon when I woke up the next day. I got up and came out of my bedroom and peeped into Kim's bedroom but she wasn't there. That's when I looked at the clock and saw that it was almost noon. I couldn't ever remember sleeping that late before. That bus trip really wore me out. I went into the bathroom, washed up and got dressed. Sarah heard me stirring and came into my room. "Good morning," she said.

"Good morning."

"Did you sleep well?"

"Do you have any doubt? Look at the time."

"Yes, I was hoping that you woke up before I had to pick Kim up from preschool."

"I'm surprised that I didn't hear you getting her up."

"That's because she got up in the middle of the night and got in the bed with Sam and me. After you get some breakfast, we'll ride around a while before I have to pick her up. She didn't want to go but I would've had to pay anyway, so I took her. This way I can have some time alone with you."

I followed Sarah out to the kitchen. "Corn flakes is good enough for me. I want to see the Strip. I want to see what all the talk of the Las Vegas Strip is about."

"We can go. But it's better to see the Strip at night." I ate my corn flakes fast and we left the house.

The Strip was beautiful to me even in the daytime. We rode to the very end and then turned around and rode downtown and onto the Westside. She took me by the night club on the Westside where she met Sam. She told me that she met Sam through John and Ruth. "They were married first. I knew Ruth from Compton and when I came to Las Vegas to visit her and John, they introduced me to Sam. Sam and John were both in the Air Force. Three months later, Sam and I were married and I moved to Las Vegas." We rode and looked at the sights until it was time to pick Kim up.

When we picked Kim up, she gave me a clay plaque that she had made in preschool. We went back home and rested awhile before we left to go to the Allen's house. Hattie and her mother were home when we got there. When Hattie answered the door, I was glad to see that she was taller than me. The last time I measured myself, I was 5'8" so Hattie had to be at least 5'11. She was thin and reasonably attractive. But she was not as attractive as she obviously thought she was. I had her pegged right away, trying to talk all proper. We walked in and Sarah introduced us. She greeted me and called out, "Mother."

Ruth came rushing into the living room and Sarah introduced me to her. "She looks just like you," Ruth said to Sarah.

"Really?" The comment seemed to have made her happy.

"You all come on in," Ruth said, and we all followed her out to the kitchen.

Their house was large and nice too. But, I liked Sarah's taste in furniture better. Ruth went on with her cooking and we all stayed in the kitchen with her and talked until Sarah got up from the table and went over to the sink where Ruth was. She said something to Ruth in Pig-Latin and Ruth answered her back in Pig-Latin. They started laughing and Hattie said, "Uh-oh, it's time to go Mossy. Kim do you want some ice cream?"

"Yes," Kim answered excitedly.

Hattie got up and got a bowl and gave Kim some ice cream from the freezer. Then she said, "Come on Mossy, let's go talk in my bedroom." I got up and followed her to her bedroom.

When we got in her room, she took some clothes out of her chair and I sat down. She sat on her bed facing me.

"Well, how do you like Henderson so far?"

"As far as I can tell, it's great. As soon as I get use to this dry heat, I'll like it better."

"Pretty soon you won't even notice it. You see, we're sitting down in this valley with the mountains all around us and that's why the air is so dry. Are you going to be ready to take the LPN test next Monday? I know that Mrs. Martin told you that I signed you up."

"Yes she did and I really do appreciate it. But on the question of if I'm ready, I don't know. I haven't had anything to study for it. Have you been studying?"

"No I haven't. And if I did have a book, I wouldn't study it. I don't care whether I pass that test or not. This is Mama's and Mrs. Martin's idea. Me, I'd rather be a go-go dancer or work in a night club. I want to live my life in the limelight, not cooped up on a hospital ward. I will have to take you out one night and let you see those girls shake their asses. Do you like stuff like that?"

"I have never seen anything like that, but it sounds like something that I'd like. When can we go?"

"We will have to feel it out. My parents and Mr. and Mrs. Martin can't know. Daddy would ground me if he found out. Did you see my car outside?"

"Yes, it's beautiful."

"I'm driving you to Las Vegas to take the test."

"Oh, thank you. I think Sarah told me that you were driving us."

We visited for a little over an hour. In that time, I had already heard about her car, credit card, more shoes than she could count and more clothes than she could wear. I was glad when Kim came to her bedroom door and announced that Sarah was ready to leave. I got up right away and followed Kim back to where Sarah and Ruth were. We said our "so longs" and "see you laters" and left.

On the way home, Sarah asked me, "Well what do you think?"

"About Hattie?"

"Yes, but if it's bad, you can tell me later because somebody is listening."

She made a gesture with her head towards Kim.

"Besides the bragging, she's okay I guess."

"Ruth is hoping that the two of you can be friends."

"It's too soon for me to tell about that. She seems fake."

"Nobody is what they seem to be at first." I didn't understand the statement, so I didn't respond.

When we got home, Sam was home and had started dinner. Sarah and I finished it. During dinner, I was careful not to make any bloops and blunders at the table. After dinner, Sam went to the family room and took Kim with him. Sarah and I cleaned up the kitchen and talked. I didn't tell her that Hattie didn't want to be a nurse anymore than I did. When we were through in the kitchen, I watched television in my room and Kim joined me. She stayed with me until bedtime.

Sarah and I spent a lot of time together during the week that she was off. We shopped, went sight seeing, talked and ate out. I visited with Hattie just about every evening before we took the test. When I met her father John, I could see where she had gotten her height from. He was 6'5". Sarah said that they called him high pockets when he was in the military. Hattie favored her father and she even bragged about that. "It's good luck for a girl to favor her father and for a boy to favor his mother." she said.

It wouldn't be very lucky if your mother and father looked like hounds, I thought.

The Sunday before the test, Hattie and I attended church with our families and then went to the movies that evening. When she dropped me off, she told me to be ready at 6:30 a.m. the next morning. I took my bath before I went to bed and I set my alarm clock for 5:30 a.m. The next morning, I jumped out of bed as soon as the alarm went off. I washed up, got dressed and forced down a slice of toast and a glass of orange juice. At 6:30 a.m., Hattie knocked on the door and I hollered, "I'm coming."

I rushed out, locked the door and we took off for Las Vegas. It took us at least forty minutes to get to the test site. We were the first ones there, so she parked as close to the entrance as possible and we sat and talked. On the way we had started talking about sneaking into the night clubs, so we finished the conversation. "I'm glad that you're tall like me," she said. "We can dress in black and avoid getting carded. I've been going in night clubs for a year now and I haven't been carded yet. I used to worry about being tall because all of the cute guys are short, but I found out that there is an advantage in being tall. I get away with a lot. Since it's only me, my parents are glad that I'm tall so I can protect myself. And anyway, I can still get any man that I want, short or tall. In fact, a short man likes to be seen with a tall woman. It makes them feel macho. To tell you the truth, I like making out with short guys better because they really try hard to please you. They don't just slam, bam, thank you ma'am like the tall ones."

I was leaning back looking straight ahead, but when she said that I looked at her.

"Why are you looking at me like that? Haven't you made out on the back seat of a car?"

"No, not really."

"Well I sure have. I made this one dude kick the window out of his car. I would have probably made him tear up his car, but I didn't have enough room on the back seat and I couldn't move fast enough."

We started laughing and I sat straight up just as another car pulled up. The two people talked for a while and then the girl got out and the man drove away. The girl walked up to the school and stood on the steps. I watched her while Hattie was talking. She was saying something about, "I could tell you some stories that would make your hair curl."

There was something about this girl's mannerism that caught my attention. *That's the prettiest girl that I've ever seen. Not flashy, just plain and pretty.*

"Let's get out and wait with that girl," I said to Hattie.

"Why don't we invite her to sit in the car with us?"

"We don't know her name. What are we going to say? Hey You?"

"Okay let's get out. It's almost eight o'clock anyway." So we got out of the car, walked over, said good morning and introduced ourselves.

Hattie went first. "I'm Hattie Jean Allen," she said and extended her hand.

The girl shook her hand and answered, "I'm Meredith Jones and I'm pleased to meet you."

"I'm Mossy Lewis," I said and extended my hand.

She smiled and shook my hand. "I'm pleased to meet you Mossy."

"Are you ready for this test?" I asked.

"I don't know. I'm just going to do my best."

"That's all any of us can do," Hattie said. "Was that your father who dropped you off?"

Meredith laughed and said, "No, that's my brother and I'm glad that he didn't hear you calling him my father."

"From what I could tell, he's cute," Hattie said.

Meredith just smiled, but she didn't respond. Hattie kept talking to Meredith, mostly asking her questions. I couldn't get a word in edge-wise, so I just stood listening to Hattie playing twenty questions with her.

A crowd had gathered and the proctor and her helper came and opened the door and let us in. I was planning to sit beside Meredith, but Hattie questioned her all the way into the testing room and sat down beside her. Somebody else sat on the other side of Meredith so I sat next to Hattie. I heard Meredith tell Hattie that she wasn't really worried about the test because she had a lead on a nurse's aide job and I wanted to talk to her about it.

When the test started, I worked hard to finish before Hattie and Meredith so I could wait outside to ask her more about the nurse's aide job. We were told when we were finished with our test paper to turn it in and leave quietly by the side door. I was doing well until Hattie and a lot of the others started leaving. That made me nervous because I didn't want to be the last to leave. The test questions were multiple choice, so I answered all of mine "C" and turned my papers in and left. When Hattie saw me coming out, she met me and said, "The test was a piece of cake, wasn't it?"

"Yes, it was pretty easy."

"Are you ready to go?"

"I would like to wait for Meredith. I want to find out about the job that she was telling you about."

"That job that she's talking about is for a nurse's aide. That's the same as being a maid. You don't want to do that, we're going to be LPNs."

"I still want to talk to her. There is something about her that I like. She favors my sister Ellen."

"Okay, we'll wait."

When Meredith came out, I met her and asked, "Well how did you do?"

"I don't know. That test looked like Greek to me." We laughed.

"You really think so?" Hattie asked. "I thought that it was pretty simple."

"How do you think you did?" Meredith asked me.

"I did all right I think. I completed most of them. You know you favor my sister who's next to me."

"I'll take that as a compliment," Meredith answered with a smile.

"I would like to get together and talk," I said.

"That would be great. I haven't met anybody to talk to since I got here. I'll give you my telephone number and you can call me. If my sister answers grouchy, don't let it discourage you, just ask for me."

She wrote her phone number on a piece of paper and gave it to me. I took a piece of paper from my purse, gave her my phone number and promised to call her. We said so long and she started walking away. "How are you getting home?" Hattie called to her. "Is your brother picking you up?"

"No. He had to go to work. I'm taking the bus."

"Come on, I'll give you a ride," Hattie said.

"No thanks. I'm not going straight home."

"Wait a minute," I called to her and ran over to her. Hattie didn't follow me and I was glad. "When are you going to apply for that nurse's aide job?"

"Today, while I'm off from work."

"Where is it? I would like to apply too, if you don't mind. Maybe we can work together."

"All right," she said, smiling from ear to ear. And she told me the name of the hospital that she was applying at. "I know a lady who has a niece who works there."

"If you can wait until tomorrow morning, I'll meet you there and apply too."

"It will mean taking another day off from work, but I'll do it if you're really sure you'll be there."

"I will, I promise."

"Okay, I'll see you at nine o'clock tomorrow morning."

"See ya," I answered and walked back to where Hattie was.

"What were you guys talking about?"

"Nothing important." We got in her car and left.

On the way, Hattie told me more about her car escapades. But I was barely listening. I had more important things on my mind. I had no idea that my life was about to get real complicated.

www.ingramcontent.com/pod-product-compliance
Lightning Source LLC
LaVergne TN
LVHW010058110826
845155LV00028B/395